HUMAN NATURE

SCREENPLAY AND INTERVIEW

CHARLIE KAUFMAN

A Newmarket Shooting Script® Series Book

NEWMARKET PRESS • NEW YORK

This book is published simultaneously in the United States of America and in Canada.

FIRST EDITION

02 03 04 10 9 8 7 6 5 4 3 2 1

ISBN: 1-55704-509-7 (paperback)

Library of Congress Catalog-in-Publication Data is available upon request.

QUANTITY PURCHASES

Companies, professional groups, clubs, and other organizations may qualify for special terms when ordering quantities of this title. For information, write to Special Sales, Newmarket Press, 18 East 48th Street, New York, NY 10017; call (212) 832-3575 or 1-800-669-3903; FAX (212) 832-3629; or email mailbox@newmarketpress.com.
Website: www.newmarketpress.com

Manufactured in the United States of America.

OTHER BOOKS IN THE NEWMARKET SHOOTING SCRIPT® SERIES INCLUDE:

The Age of Innocence: The Shooting Script
American Beauty: The Shooting Script
The Birdcage: The Shooting Script
Cast Away: The Shooting Script
Dead Man Walking: The Shooting Script
Erin Brockovich: The Shooting Script
Gosford Park: The Shooting Script
Gods and Monsters: The Shooting Script
The Ice Storm: The Shooting Script
Knight's Tale: The Shooting Script
Man on the Moon: The Shooting Script
The Matrix: The Shooting Script
Nurse Betty: The Shooting Script
The People vs. Larry Flynt: The Shooting Script
The Shawshank Redemption: The Shooting Script
Snatch: The Shooting Script
Snow Falling on Cedars: The Shooting Script
State and Main: The Shooting Script
Traffic: The Shooting Script
The Truman Show: The Shooting Script

OTHER NEWMARKET PICTORIAL MOVIEBOOKS AND NEWMARKET INSIDER FILM BOOKS INCLUDE:

The Age of Innocence: A Portrait of the Film★
ALI: The Movie and The Man★
Amistad: A Celebration of the Film by Steven Spielberg
The Art of The Matrix★
Bram Stoker's Dracula: The Film and the Legend★
Cradle Will Rock: The Movie and the Moment★
Crouching Tiger, Hidden Dragon: A Portrait of the Ang Lee Film★
Dances with Wolves: The Illustrated Story of the Epic Film★
Gladiator: The Making of the Ridley Scott Epic Film
The Jaws Log
Men in Black: The Script and the Story Behind the Film★
Neil Simon's Lost in Yonkers: The Illustrated Screenplay of the Film★
Planet of The Apes: Re-imagined by Tim Burton★
Saving Private Ryan: The Men, The Mission, The Movie
The Sense and Sensibility Screenplay & Diaries★
The Seven Years in Tibet Screenplay and Story★
Stuart Little: The Art, the Artists and the Story Behind the Amazing Movie★

★*Includes Screenplay*

CONTENTS

HUMAN NATURE

Written by Charlie Kaufman

FADE IN:

EXT. FOREST - DAY

Shots of wildlife: grazing deer, a hawk in a tree, bees buzzing around flowers, a spider building a web. Then, from far away: a tense discussion, a scuffle, an ear-splitting gunshot. The hawk screams and flies from its perch high into the sky. The deer bolts, jumps a log, tears through the half built spiderweb. The spider falls to the forest floor. Two mice appear from under the log and run for their lives. The hawk, circling and surveying the scene below, spots the mice, now running through a clearing. It swoops, closing in on them. The mice exchange glances, then, at the last second, split up, running on either side of a large tree. The hawk smashes into the tree with a "thonk", drops to the ground, and staggers, dazed, past the prostrate body of a dead man.

INT. INTERROGATION ROOM - DAY

EXTREME CLOSE-UP OF LILA TALKING TO THE CAMERA

LILA
I'm not sorry.

A bead of sweat trickles down her cheek. Then: a blinding flash of light obliterates her face.

INT. CONGRESS - DAY

EXTREME CLOSE-UP OF PUFF TALKING TO THE CAMERA

PUFF
I am sorry.

A tear wells in Puff's eye and runs down his face. Another blinding flash of light.

INT. WHITE SPACE - DAY

EXTREME CLOSE-UP OF NATHAN TALKING TO THE CAMERA

NATHAN
I don't even know what sorry means anymore.

As Nathan speaks, a trickle of blood drips down his face from his out-of-frame forehead. Another blinding flash of light.

EXT. POLICE STATION - NIGHT

It's a frenetic hand-held shot as Lila is pulled from a police car and dragged into the precinct house. Cameras flash. Reporters shout questions.

(CONTINUED)

CONTINUED:

Lila attempts to shield her face from view, but she is handcuffed and can only manage to hunch her shoulders.

INT. INTERROGATION ROOM - NIGHT

A ratty interrogation room. Institutional green walls. Beat-up file cabinets. Lila, thirties, sits at the end of a long table. A tape recorder whirs in front of her. She is smoking. Three-fat, mean-looking cops sit at the other end of the table. One of the cops eyes her lasciviously. Lila's hand shakes as she brings the cigarette to her mouth.

LILA
I'm not sorry. So I spend the rest of my life in jail. I've been in jail my whole life anyway. A jail of blood and tissue and coursing hormones...

One of the cops sighs and massages the bridge of his nose. It's going to be a long night.

LILA (CONT'D)
... A jail called the human body.

The lascivious cop smiles lasciviously at Lila's reference to "human body." He looks her up and down.

LILA (CONT'D)
My soul held prisoner in this reeking, stench-ridden bag of bones and entrails. A bag of feces and piss and fibroid cysts in my tits and pre-cancerous moles on my sun-damaged back...

The lascivious cop gags a little, repulsed. Lila drags on her cigarette, calmer now.

LILA (CONT'D)
At least now I'll be able to blame the state, not God, for my incarceration.

INT. CONGRESS - DAY

Puff thirties, dirty, scraggly hair and beard but in a crisp business suit, testifies before a congressional committee. The auditorium is filled with reporters and spectators. Puff sits in front of a microphone, counsel at his side. He pours himself a glass of water, drinks, clears his throat, then speaks: stentorian, confident.

PUFF
I am sorry, gentlemen, sorry for all of us. Yours is a complicated, sad world.

CONTINUED:

This is a revelation to the assembled crowd. People whisper to each other.

PUFF (CONT'D)
I was living a life of simplicity when I was ripped from my Eden and immersed in this harshness. Some would argue the life I was living was not a human life at all. And, gentlemen, I don't have a clever retort. I am not a philosopher. The only thing I know is that I am sorry, sorry for my expulsion, sorry for my Lila rotting in her jail cell, and sorry for Nathan ... rotting in his grave.

INT. WHITE SPACE - DAY

Nathan, thirties, in a white robe, sits alone at a white table. Everything is white except for an oozing bullet wound in Nathan's temple.

NATHAN
I don't even know what sorry means anymore. It's odd. When I was alive I knew -- maybe it was all I knew -- but here sorry is meaningless. Love is meaningless. Jealousy is meaningless. Ambition... meaningless. Everything that motivated my every breath while I was alive is now meaningless.
(beat)
I guess that's how I can be sure I'm really dead.

INT. INTERROGATION ROOM - NIGHT

Lila watches the tape recorder. The cops are sipping coffee. Lila looks at them.

LILA
My story begins when I was twelve.

COP
(Checks watch)
Jesus.

EXT. SCHOOL STREET - DAY

It's got that faded, "memory" look. Twelve-year old Lila hurries home from school, books clutched to her chest. Other kids walk along the street in pairs or groups, laughing and chatting. Lila walks alone, a worried scowl on her face.

(CONTINUED)

CONTINUED:

LILA (V.O.)
Something terrible happened that year.

INT. YOUNG LILA'S HOUSE - DAY

Colors are still muted. It looks to be somewhere in the early 70's based on the preponderance of Bay City Rollers posters on the wall. Twelve-year-old Lila enters the room, closes the door, locks it, and rattles the doorknob to make sure the door is really locked. She draws the shades. She pulls some T-shirts from her dresser drawer and stuffs them into the space between the bottom of the door and the floor.

KID BROTHER (O.S.)
(Muffled)
Hey, no fair!

TWELVE YEAR OLD LILA

Drop dead, Eric. Lila stands nervously in front of the full-length mirror on her closet door. She takes a deep breath and begins to unbutton her shirt, watching herself carefully in the mirror.

ADULT LILA (V.O.)
My mother said because of it I would never be able to get a man, I should get used to the idea of dedicating my life to the pursuit of knowledge, or religion... or whatever.

Lila's shirt is now unbuttoned. She pulls it open. She is wearing a training bra over the very beginning of breasts. On her chest above the bra, and on her stomach below it, is hair. Dark curly hair. She stares at it, touches it cautiously. Then she starts to cry. She crouches into a ball and weeps.

ADULT LILA
The doctor said...

INT. DOCTOR'S OFFICE - DAY

Old fashioned office. Twelve-year-old Lila sits on the examination table, her shirt off. An elderly male doctor touches the hair, fingers it. Her mother looks on.

DOCTOR
(To the mother)
It's hormonal. Nature is a funny and complex thing. It could get worse with time.

(CONTINUED)

CONTINUED:

Young Lila turns to the camera.

TWELVE YEAR OLD LILA

By the time I was twenty I looked like an ape.

INT. INTERROGATION ROOM - NIGHT

The cop, who gagged, gags again. Lila stares at him. Her face is hard, blank. She stubs out her cigarette.

INT. CONGRESS - DAY

Puff testifies before the committee.

PUFF
I don't think there's anyone in the world that doesn't know by now that I was raised in the wilderness by an ape.

DISSOLVE TO:

EXT. FOREST CLEARING - DAY.

This has a faded, "memory" look also. A naked, bearded, dirty middle-aged man and a naked, dirty ten-year-old Puff walk along like apes, crouched over and dragging their knuckles.

PUFF (V.O.)
Well, to be fair, by a man who thought himself an ape, but it amounts to the same thing, gentlemen, does it not?
(Sadly)
Oh, papa....

INT. PUFF'S DAD'S OFFICE- DAY

Puff's father, wearing a starched white shirt and tie, sits at a desk writing in a ledger. He is trying hard to fit in, but there is something simian about him.

PUFF (V.O.)
After spending years in a mental hospital for attempting to take up residence in the ape house of the local zoo, he did his best to live by your rules. He got a job, he married a human, and they had me.

A coworker walks by with a newspaper and Puff's father sees the headline. It reads: President Kennedy Assassinated.

CONTINUED:

PUFF (V.O) (CONT'D)
Until a national tragedy undid all those years of therapy and reminded him what the human race was truly about.

Puff's father looks heavenward, clutches at his temples in despair, jumps on top of a file cabinet, and screams.

EXT. YOUNG PUFF'S HOUSE -- NIGHT

Puff's father climbs out a second story window with a small bundle in his arms. He runs off into the night.

PUFF
So he stole little me from my human mother, and raised me, with love and tenderness and respect, as an ape like himself.

INT. CONGRESS- DAY

Puff looks pointedly at the congressman.

PUFF
Apes don't assassinate their presidents, gentlemen.

The congressmen are shamed: they look down, they take notes, they mumble instructions to the assistants seated behind them.

EXT. FOREST - DAY

An adult Puff and his now older father sit on the forest floor and pick bugs off each other and eat them.

PUFF (V.O.)
Until quite recently I believed myself to be an ape, although I didn't know specifically what type. Apes don't think in terms of type.

DISSOLVE TO:

INT. CONGRESS - DAY

Puff testifies.

PUFF
It might be argued, gentlemen, that apes don't even know they are apes. In retrospect, however, I'd say I was a pygmy chimp.

(CONTINUED)

CONTINUED:

Puff holds up an illustration of a pygmy chimp. Several reporters run from the room: a scoop!

INT. WHITE SPACE - DAY

Nathan talks to nobody in particular.

NATHAN
I have to say I always hated apes. Of course I don't any longer. Now I don't even know what hate means. But while alive, I hated apes. I blame my parents. I mean, I don't blame them. I don't know what blame is, really, anymore, but I think they influenced me in my ape-hating tendencies.

DISSOLVE TO:

EXT. ZOO - DAY

Faded colors. Ten year old Nathan in a bow tie and short-panted suit walks along with his uptight British parents. They arrive at the ape pen. Nathan is excited. He jumps up and down. The apes jump up and down also.

INTNATHAN AS A BOY
Monkeys! Look, mama, monkeys!

Nathan makes monkey noises, scratches himself.

MOTHER
(clamping down on his shoulder)
Nathan, Chimpanzees are apes, not monkeys.

Nathan becomes subdued. Finally, politely:

NATHAN AS A BOY
Thank you for the clarification, mama.

Nathan makes a note of this in a little memo pad.

MOTHER
You're very welcome.

Suddenly there is a commotion off screen. Two uniformed attendants drag Puff's father, straitjacketed and kicking and screaming like an ape, past Nathan and his parents.

PUFF'S FATHER
I am an ape, I tell you! This is my home!

(CONTINUED)

CONTINUED:

Nathan, his father, and the other zoo patrons look on curiously, a little frightened. Nathan's mother chooses to ignore it.

MOTHER
And furthermore ... Tell him, Harold.

FATHER
(distracted)
Uh ...
(then by rote)
The ape is our closest biological relative -- specifically the pygmy chimp.
(holds up the same illustration of a pygmy chimp that Puff showed the congressional committee)
A single chromosome separates us. But you know what truly separates us?

NATHAN AS A BOY
(taking notes)
Single chro-no-zone.
(looking up)
No, papa. What?

FATHER
Civilization.

Nathan scribbles in book.

NATHAN AS A BOY
Sib-ill-ih-say-shun.

FATHER
Without it, we might as well be living in pens, throwing our feces, masturbating in public ...
(beat, a reverie)
...sniffing red swollen female rump ...

The mother glares witheringly at the father and he shuts up. She pulls the notebook from Nathan's hands and crosses out the last thing he wrote, then kneels down in front of him.

MOTHER
Nathan, your adoptive father and I whisked you away from a life that most certainly would've been one of degradation and alcoholism. We did this at great personal sacrifice. You see, we only love you more because you're not our real son.

CONTINUED: (2)

NATHAN
I hope you know I appreciate it to the up-
most.

MOTHER
Utmost. So your part of the bargain is
to never wallow in the filth of instinct.
Any dumb animal can do that.

INT. INTERROGATION ROOM - NIGHT

Lila lights a new cigarette with her spent one. She drags.

LILA
Oh, I had animal urges. I had the urge
to merge, officers. Inside I was 100%
grade A female.
(laughs derisively)
But who would want someone as unladylike
as me? I did everything I could to
shield the world from my repulsiveness.

DISSOLVE TO:

INT. COLLEGE DORM BATHROOM - DAY

Stockings hang over the shower curtain rod. The window shade
is drawn. Towels are stuffed in the space under the door. A
twenty year old naked Lila is covered with shaving cream,
face to feet. She is shaving. There is a pounding on the
door.

FEMALE ROOMMATE (O.S.)
Lila, what are you doing in there? I
need to get ready for my date.

LILA
Nothing! I'll be out in a minute!

The door opens. Lila freezes.

FEMALE ROOMMATE
Look, I'll just ...
(stops in her tracks when she
sees Lila)
Oh, God...

Lila is mortified.

DISSOLVE TO:

INT. COLLEGE DORM ROOM

Lila is sitting in her bathrobe on her bed and staring out the window. There is a bit of shaving cream behind her ear. Her roommate runs back and forth, getting ready for her date.

FEMALE ROOMMATE
I don't know why you didn't tell me about this.

LILA
It's embarrassing, okay?

FEMALE ROOMMATE
It's not so bad.
(beat)
So, like, it just keeps growing?

LILA
Yeah, Natalie. It's hair. It grows.

FEMALE ROOMMATE
Well, don't jump down my throat. I'm just trying to help.

LILA
How is that helping, Natalie? How exactly?

FEMALE ROOMMATE
Look, if you're going to be like that ... You should be appreciative that I'm interested.

LILA
Why, because I'm a freak and you're beautiful, and you're nice enough to come down to my freak, non-beautiful level and act concerned about my repulsive troubles?

FEMALE ROOMMATE
(pegged)
You're fucked up, Lila.
(out the door)
Why don't you fucking try electrolysis or something? Figure it out for Christ sake.

The door slams. Lila hugs her knees to her chest.

LILA (V.O.)
At sixty dollars an hour, electrolysis was not a feasible solution. I needed another option. I remembered a painting I saw once.

INT. ART MUSEUM - DAY

Twelve year old Lila walks sadly through an art museum. She looks at various old portraits of men. She studies their facial hair. When she turns a corner, she is shocked to see a large Renaissance painting of a naked woman entirely covered with fur. She rushes to it, looks at the placard next to the painting. It's Mary Magdalen.

LILA (V.O.)
Mary Magdalen, perhaps the only sexualized female in all of Christian mythology, and here she was covered with hair. I guess that's where I got the idea maybe the Catholic Church might applaud excessive hair growth in its women.

EXT. CONVENT - DAY

Lila, in a nun's habit, is on her knees praying.

LILA
Heavenly Father ...
(sighs)
... please make this hair go away.

LILA (V.O.) (CONT'D)
But my prayers were always so selfish.

INT. LESBIAN KITCHEN - NIGHT

A whole lot of women are crowded into the room. Some sit around, some cook, some chat, some caress each other. Lila, pretty hairy, sits alone at the table eating a bowl of soup.

LILA (V.O.)
For a while being a lesbian separatist seemed an option. But, frankly... too many women.

INT. TENT - DAY

Lila, in a full beard, hangs onto a cardboard Empire State Building, in a reenactment of the scene from King Kong. A normally proportioned, yet abnormally small person, FRANK, in a cardboard biplane suspended from wires, circles Lila.

CONTINUED:

LILA (V.O.)
I became a professional circus freak.

Lila looks out at the crowd: dumb, mouth-breathing children gawk, adult men are repulsed, adult women unconsciously touch their own chins, testing for hair. It is suddenly more than Lila can bear.

INT. LILA'S BATHROOM - NIGHT

The room is lit with candles. Lila finishes shaving herself all over. Then she takes the double-edged blade out of the razor and climbs into the a bathtub filled with warm water. She is about to slice her wrists. On the shelf next to the tub a little gray mouse watches her intently. At first she is startled, but then she and the creature seem to be communing. His little black beady eyes reflect the candle light. Lila starts to cry. She puts down the blade.

INTERROGATION ROOM - NIGHT

Lila wipes a tear from her eye.

LILA
The way that mouse looked at me. It didn't care if I had hair all over my body. I was just what I was. I felt so free. Do you understand what I'm saying? The cops look up, on the spot. It seems their minds were elsewhere.

COP
Something about a mouse, right?

Lila sighs.

DISSOLVE TO:

EXT. FOREST - MORNING

A small tent. A smoking campfire. There's a rustling in the tent. Lila steps out naked. She is covered with fur. She pours a cup of coffee, and stands, comfortable in her skin, watching the world around her. Squirrels jump from tree to tree, birds look down at her. She sees a scurrying chipmunk, a skulking coyote, a cute bear cub.

(CONTINUED)

CONTINUED:

LILA
(singing)
Look at all the hair everywhere, everywhere/
On the possum and the woodchuck and the cuddly ol' bear/
I used to be embarrassed/
of hair not fit to caress/
Now I'm so sure it's a blessing/
I've got no need of dressing I once thought God/a creator diabolical/ He gave the nod/ To each one of my follicles/
head to my baby toe I was dismayed/
to see my hirsute reflection/
I'd shave each day/
with new, emollient protection/
Stubble would have to go
Now I'm free/ No more cares/ I've accepted my millions of hairs/ My new friends/ These split ends/ Far away from those terrible stares The squirrels don't mind/ a girl who's furred or clean shaven/ Creatures are kind/ So I have found my new green haven/ And I ain't gonna go/ Cause I'm one of them, you know.

Lila sighs contentedly, picks up a pad and pen from a rock, sits on the rock and writes.

LILA (V.O.) (CONT'D)
I figured a way to stay in the woods forever. I became a nature writer.

INT. BEAUTY PARLOR - DAY

A woman under a hair drier reads a book intently. We see the first sentence of the chapter: "Last night, on my mountaintop, I felt the wind whip through my hair." We hear Lila's dramatic reading competing with the very loud sound of the hair drier.

LILA (V.O.)
Last night, on my mountaintop, I felt the wind whip through my hair.

DISSOLVE TO:

EXT. FOREST - NIGHT

There is a violent, violent storm. The hair drier drone has turned into the explosive noise of rain beating down in sheets and wind howling at fifty miles an hour.

(CONTINUED)

CONTINUED:

Branches crack. Lila's tent blows over, revealing her huddled there with a sleeping bag wrapped around her like a blanket.

LILA (V.O)
It was violent. I almost died.

Lightning hits a tree nearby. It falls with a smack practically on top of Lila. She screams, then defiantly stands, throwing off the sleeping bag. The wind and rain whip her hair around her head. She laughs with gusto and raises her arms like a runner winning a marathon.

LILA (V.O.) (CONT'D)
All my petty concerns were sent flying with those gale force winds. I was in nature. I was nature: an otter, a stork, an oak tree. A woman. Alive... for the moment anyway. And as Nietzche said, what does not kill me makes me stronger. That goes double if you're a woman.

EXT. BOOK STORE WINDOW - DAY

We see many copies of a book entitled "Wind in my Hair" by Lila Jute.

LILA (V.O.)
I became a successful nature writer.

INT. BEAUTY PARLOR - DAY

We see a woman under a hair drier reading "Wind in my Hair". We pull back to see that a long row of women under hair dryers are reading Lila's book. They all stand defiantly, proudly, knocking their hair dryers up and back as they do. The blowing hair dryers whip the women's wet hair around their heads. The multiple hair drier drone is unbearably loud.

LILA (V.O.)
When I became a famous nature writer, I said to myself, fuck humanity ...

INT. BOOKSTORE WINDOW - DAY

A big display of the book "Fuck Humanity" by Lila Jute. A long line of women with beautifully coiffured hair snakes toward the cash register.

CONTINUED:

LILA (V.O.)
... I never saw my public, I never saw my publisher, I never saw another human being.

DISSOLVE TO:

INT. LOG HOUSE - DAY

Lila lies in bed typing on a lap top. A dog lies with her and licks her knee. She seems to enjoy it, and gets lost in a reverie. The dog becomes a handsome man, kissing her knee and working his way up her thigh and under her nightgown. Lila is getting seriously hot and bothered. Her head lolls. But the reverie dissipates and the man turns back into a dog rooting around her crotch with his cold nose. She pushes him away. The dejected dog gets off the bed.

LILA (V.O.)
By the time I was thirty I was very, very horny. Lila gets out of bed and studies herself in the mirror.

She brushes her hands against her hairy body.

LILA (V.O.) (CONT'D)
I had to have a man in my... life. I would become what I needed to become to achieve this. I would become a hairless lie.

The mirror image of Lila shimmers and turns into Lila with no body hair. Lila all made-up and with a smart new hairstyle. She assumes a coquettish pose and smiles cutely at herself.

INT. INTERROGATION ROOM - NIGHT

Lila talks. One of the cops is doodling. One is picking wax from his ear with a pencil. One is reading a paperback novel under the table.

LILA
This is when everything changed, and this is where my confession really begins.

The cops look up.

INT. ELECTROLOGIST'S OFFICE - DAY

Lila lies shirtless on a table while LOUISE, her fifty year old electrologist, works on her back.

(CONTINUED)

CONTINUED:

LOUISE
Progress!

LILA
Ouch. Yeah?

LOUISE
Oh yeah, honey. Getting smooth smooth smooth all over. Smooth as a baby's butt.

LILA
I love it, Louise. I'm getting to be a real girl.

LOUISE
You still in the market for a real boy?

LILA
Always. Ow.

LOUISE
(beat)
Cause there's this guy. My brother knows him. Might be right up your alley.

LILA
Tell me. I could use someone up my alley.

LOUISE
(playing dumb)
I don't get that. Is that sexual?

LILA
Shut up and tell me.

LOUISE
Handsome, thirties, psychologist ...

LILA
Loves animals? Ouch. Must love animals, Louise.

LOUISE
Loves animals. Loves you.

LILA
What do you mean?

LOUISE
Somehow it came up that you were a friend of mine.
(MORE)

(CONTINUED)

LOUISE (CONT'D)
Mr. handsome, animal-loving psychologist said he would love to meet you.

LILA
Holy shit. Your brother didn't tell him the nature of our relationship, did he?

LOUISE
My brother is discreet.

LILA
(rubbing hand across jaw)
Won't he be able to tell?

LOUISE
My brother says the guy's a thirty-five year old virgin, so maybe he won't know how women usually feel. Plus he's got bad eyesight, almost legally blind, which is helpful in this situation. Plus he's got an extremely small penis, of which he is "mortifyingly ashamed." Chances are he'll be so grateful for any non-judgmental attention, he'll be yours forever.

LILA
He must be really close to your brother to tell him such personal stuff.

LOUISE
Yeah. My brother is his shrink.

INT. RESTAURANT - NIGHT

It's a chi-chi place. Lila sits at a table with Nathan, fastidious in dress and manner. There is an awkward first-date silence. She sneaks a glance at his crotch. Then:

NATHAN
Meditations on a Banana Slug was a delightful read.

LILA
Thank you so much. I love slugs. All slugs, not just banana slugs.

NATHAN
As do I.

LILA
They're even keel. Forging ahead with slow determination. They don't get distracted or side-tracked.
(MORE)

CONTINUED:

LILA (CONT'D)
Don't care what they look like. They don't care that people see them and go, "Ewww. A slug."

NATHAN
They don't seem to be especially ego driven, this is true.

LILA
You've got to respect that.

NATHAN
I have to say, I'm not there yet.

LILA
Where?

NATHAN
Slugdom. Sluggishness. Whatever you'd call it. I'm not there yet. I still have many human characteristics.

LILA
That's not necessarily a bad thing.

NATHAN
I suppose not. But still. One would like to move beyond.

LILA
I'm not sure we can escape our natures. Believe me I've tried. I'm not even so sure anymore that we should want to.

NATHAN
I love that you said that. It makes me feel a bit lighter. I've been rather heavy lately. Thinking about my childhood. Realizing how much a product I am of my upbringing.
(beat, cautiously)
I've been seeing someone. A therapist.

LILA
(feigning surprise)
You are a therapist, right?

NATHAN
No, no. I'm a psychologist, but I do research. I'm a behaviorist. I work with animals. Mice at the moment.

LILA
I hope you don't perform any of those dreadful torture experiments, Nathan.

NATHAN
Heavens no. My work now is ... Right now I'm teaching mice ... well, table manners, to be candid.

LILA
(doesn't know what to say)
How's it going?

NATHAN
Quite well, really. A lot of work. A lot of reinforcement, mostly positive. Right now I've gotten two of my subjects to use napkins. Tiny napkins, of course.

LILA
Paper or cloth?

NATHAN
I hope you don't think me daft. It's important work. It's part of a larger sociological experiment. I'm federally funded.

LILA
What's the larger experiment?

NATHAN
It's my thesis that if table manners can be taught to mice, they can be taught to humans.

LILA
Going out on a limb, aren't you, Nathan?

NATHAN
(speech)
The truth is most people don't have table manners today. And when the foundations of civilized society crumble and disappear, civilized society in its entirety follows closely at its heels.

LILA
I'm not sure.

NATHAN
(stridently)
Courtesy, decorum, manners, are all sadly lacking from our daily intercourse. Rudeness and vulgarity are the norm.

LILA
We are animals after all.

NATHAN
Ergo if I can teach table manners to mice, I can teach them to humans. If I can teach table manners to humans, maybe I can make this world a little bit safer. For the children. For children.

Nathan blushes. Lila stares at him for a long moment. Her thoughts are unreadable.

INT. ELECTROLOGIST'S OFFICE - DAY

Lila lies on her back. Louise works on her breasts.

LOUISE
So?

LILA
I really like him, Louise. He's so ...
(searching)
... passionate about his work.

LOUISE
My brother says he likes you, too.

LILA
(pleased)
He told you that?

LOUISE
Yup. Neither of us could sleep last night, so we just laid there gabbing till God knows when.

LILA
(beat)
You sleep in the same bed with your brother?

LOUISE
No. I mean, just until his room is painted. We have a small place.

CONTINUED:

LILA
Oh.

Lila glances at several framed photos on the wall: all of Louise and her brother together in various vacation spots.

LOUISE
Anyway... Wendell says Nathan likes you even more than he likes his own mother. And according to my brother, Nathan's abnormally close with his mother.

INT. WHITE SPACE - DAY

Nathan talks.

NATHAN
I began going to a therapist when I was in my thirties, because I had vague feelings of being straightjacketed, repressed, disconnected, numb, lost... dead.
(beat)
After a time my childhood came up.

DISSOLVE TO:

INT. NATHAN'S PARENTS' HOUSE- DAY

It is another sepia scene. Nathan as a ten year old sits at the table with his parents. There is a bowl of salad in front of each of them. Everyone's head is bowed in prayer.

FATHER
Lord, we thank you for this bountiful gift we are about to receive.

ALL
Amen.

Eyes open, and young Nathan reaches for a fork to eat the salad. The wrong fork. His mother's eyes widen in horror.

MOTHER
My God, no! My God!
(disappointed)
Oh, Nathan.

Nathan looks up.

(CONTINUED)

CONTINUED:

MOTHER (CONT'D)
That is the wrong fork, young man.
(to father)
Harold, tell the boy.

FATHER
That's the wrong fork, Nathan.

NATHAN AS A BOY
(panicky)
I'll use the right one. I'm sorry. I forgot.

MOTHER
Harold, tell the boy.

FATHER
Too late. You have to go to your room.

NATHAN AS A BOY
But ...

MOTHER
Nathan, don't ask us to treat our vow to elevate you casually.

NATHAN AS A BOY
Okay. Thank you for not.

Nathan gets up, pushes in his chair and leaves the room.

DISSOLVE TO:

INT. THERAPIST'S OFFICE - DAY

Adult Nathan sits on the couch, dabbing at his eyes. Wendall, his therapist, sits across from him and writes something in his notebook.

WENDALL
And do you think maybe this early childhood indoctrination has something to do with your interest in table manners in the present?

Nathan thinks long and hard about this.

NATHAN
That seems a tad convenient, don't you think, Wendall? Wendall nods.

WENDALL
Well, do you have any thoughts then on where this passion might've come from?

NATHAN
It's my work. You can't reduce my passion to parental indoctrination. Why did Picasso paint? Why did Mozart compose?

WENDALL
Picasso's father was a painter. Mozart's father was a musician.

NATHAN
Yes, okay. Now you're just being nasty, Wendall. Now you're just showing off. I really didn't come here to be mocked.

WENDALL
That was certainly not my intention.

NATHAN
Okay.
(beat)
It's my work, Wendall. That's all.

INT. LAB - DAY

Everything's white. People in lab coats hustle back and forth. Nathan, also in a lab coat, is hovering over a Lucite encasement. Inside we see two white mice, both attached to electrodes. They sit in little chairs at a little table. In front of each of them is a little plate of salad and three forks of varying size under Lucite domes. Nathan nods to his pretty French assistant, Gabrielle, who presses a button. The Lucite domes lift. Tentatively both mice reach for a fork. There is a tiny piece of Velcro on each mouse's paw and a tiny piece of Velcro on each of the forks. The first mouse picks the correct fork, stabs it into the salad, and eats happily, relieved. The second mouse picks the wrong fork. Nathan presses a button, which sends the mouse flying off his chair with an electric shock. The correct mouse keeps eating, unconcerned. Nathan makes a note in his notebook. Gabrielle watches Nathan as he writes, enchanted.

INT. NATHAN'S APT - NIGHT

The table is elegantly set, candlelit. Lila sits at it while Nathan fusses in the kitchenette. Something classical wafts over from the stereo in the living room. Nathan places a salad in front of Lila and sits across from her with his own salad.

CONTINUED:

LILA
It looks wonderful.

NATHAN
You look wonderful. I'm on top of the world tonight, Lila. Work is going splendidly and my personal life is ...

Lila picks up a fork from the inside of her setting, not the outside. Nathan blinks. Lila tastes the salad.

LILA
Um-mmm. Oh Nathan, this salad is delish ...

NATHAN
(clenched teeth)
The fork. The fork.

LILA
I'm sorry?

NATHAN
(strangely)
Tell her, Harold ...
(stops himself)
It's just that ... It's nothing. It's just that the outside fork is usually the salad fork. One goes from the outside in.

LILA
Oh, I'm sorry.
(picks up correct fork)
I'm sorry, Nathan. I never really learned those things.

NATHAN
(forced casual)
No biggie.

There is a long silence as they both eat the salad.

LILA
Boy, this is good!

NATHAN
I'm sorry I became so upset.

LILA
No, I'm sorry. I'm really backward in certain areas.

(CONTINUED)

CONTINUED: (2)

NATHAN
(beat, blurting)
It's only that I really enjoy your company and ...

LILA
You do?

NATHAN
Yes, and ...

LILA
You really enjoy my company?

NATHAN
Yes.
(beat, blurting)
Please don't talk with food in your mouth, Lila. Please. You're so pretty and it only mars your ... I'm sorry. I'm being critical.

Nathan pounds his forehead with his fist. Lila waves her hand to indicate that it's fine. She doesn't say anything because she's chewing.

NATHAN (CONT'D)
It's just that I have some peculiarities, and --

LILA
I can't believe you think I'm pretty. I think you're pretty, too, Nathan.

NATHAN
You do?

LILA
I really do.
(beat)
But I have some peculiarities also.

NATHAN
(happily)
I don't care. I don't care!
(then, concerned)
Like what, for example?

Lila takes a deep breath, about to go into it, thinks better of it.

LILA
Like nothing.

CONTINUED: (3)

Nathan smiles, relieved. Lila smiles back. Nathan recoils slightly, skittishly half-points to his bared teeth. Apparently there's a piece of food stuck in Lila's teeth. She closes her mouth, runs her tongue over her teeth, smiles again, mouth closed.

INT. ELECTROLOGIST'S OFFICE -DAY

Louise is doing Lila's feet.

LOUISE
My brother says things are going really well between you and Nathan.

LILA
I cannot believe how in love I am with this man.

LOUISE
Yeah?

LILA
Oh, Louise, he's so cute. Even his little penis, like a little pig's penis or something. It's charming.

LOUISE
You've always been an animal lover.

LILA
He's gonna find out, Louise.

LOUISE
You're a wonderful woman. He's lucky to have you.

LILA
Louise, c'mon. You're removing hair from my feet as you say that.

LOUISE
So you've got a physical... quirk. Big deal. I'll tell you what I fall in love with in a guy: his mind. Period.

LILA
But, Louise, there's --

LOUISE
Period. End of sentence, end of paragraph, close the book, we're done. Give me a man of intellect. Like my brother, for instance.
(MORE)

(CONTINUED)

CONTINUED:

LOUISE (CONT'D)
He's average looking, but he's so smart. Y'know? I could care less about the packaging. You don't fuck the packaging.

LILA
Yeah you do.

LOUISE
You fuck the mind, Lila. You fuck the mind. Period. Close the book, end of sentence, close the...

Louise loses track.

LILA
Hey, I have a really smart friend for you. One-seventy I.Q.

LOUISE
What's he look like?

LILA
He's gorgeous. He's sort of a midget.

LOUISE
Jesus, Lila, I'm not dating a fucking midget.

INT. WHITE SPACE - DAY

Nathan talks.

NATHAN
Did I love Lila? I thought so. But what is love? Can it exist without attraction? From my new vantage point I realize love is nothing more than a messy conglomeration of need, desperation, fear of death, and insecurity about penis size. But, I'm not judging it. I know how miserable it is to be alive and...
(puts head in hands. Beat. looks up)
Listen, I don't want to be dead yet. Is there any way to ...

Nathan looks around for some sign of another person. There is nobody.

NATHAN (CONT'D)
No I suppose not.
(beat)
No biggie. Anyway, Lila moved in.
(MORE)

CONTINUED:

NATHAN (CONT'D)
We had our problems, but we both wanted love so badly, we turned a blind eye. Like the first time I brought Lila to meet my parents.

INT. NATHAN'S PARENTS' HOUSE - NIGHT

Nathan, Lila, Nathan's parents, and a six year old boy sit at the dining room table. Nathan's father leads the group in grace as Nathan shoots sideways glances at the little boy.

FATHER
Lord we thank you for this bountiful gift we are about to receive.

ALL
Amen.

Salad is about to be eaten. Everyone reaches for the correct fork and watches Lila at he same time. She touches the wrong fork, corrects herself and picks the salad fork. Nathan breathes a sigh of relief. His mother looks disappointed, clucks. They eat in silence. Finally:

LILA
It's lovely to finally meet you, Mr. and Mrs. Bronfman. I've heard so much about you from Nathan. All good, of course!

Lila laughs a little hysterically.

MOTHER
Thank you, dear.

There's a silence.

LILA
Mmmm, this salad is delicious! I just have to ask, is it lemon zest in the dressing?

MOTHER
Yes, I used three --

NATHAN
(blurting)
I'm sorry but will somebody please tell me who this little boy is.

MOTHER
Nathan!
(to Lila)
I used three lemon peels, dear, and --

CONTINUED:

NATHAN
I apologize if I sound testy, mother.
It's just a little disconcerting not to
be introduced and --

MOTHER
Wayne. His name is Wayne. Okay?

Nathan waits for more, none is forthcoming.

LILA
Well, hi, Wayne!

WAYNE
Hi, lady.

NATHAN
And Wayne is... who?

MOTHER
Your father and I have adopted an
additional son. Nathan and Wayne stare at
each other.

MOTHER (CONT'D)
Wayne just returned from a week at peace
camp and a week at science camp. Tell
everyone what you learned, Wayne.

WAYNE
Conflict resolution and flatworm
dissection.

Nathan is silent for a moment.

NATHAN
(icily)
Very nice to meet you, Wayne.

WAYNE
Nice to meet you. Our mom's told me so
much about you.

NATHAN
Yes, well, I wish I could say the same.
(to mother)
By the way, his elbow's on the table.

The mother looks over as Wayne pulls his elbow off the table.

MOTHER
Good boy.

(CONTINUED)

NATHAN
Good boy? That's it? Good boy?

FATHER
Nathan, don't talk to your mother in that tone of voice.

NATHAN
Forgive me, but it seems to me that Wayne needs a tad more --

WAYNE
Sorry, mom. I don't know where my head was.

MOTHER
Everyone makes mistakes, dear.
(to Nathan)
Wayne is quite self-disciplined for his age.

NATHAN
Meaning?

LILA
(missing the tension)
He does seem very disciplined, but I wonder, is it really the best thing for a child to be so --

The mother's eyes turn fiery as Lila talks. Nathan crazily jumps in to douse the flames.

NATHAN
Lila's a nature writer, mother! She writes about animals and nature and many other things about nature in addition to that. Wind, animals, what have you.
(beat)
Squirrels.

MOTHER
(after a long silence)
Yes, well, I love nature. As long as it stays in the zoo where it belongs. The father and Nathan laugh at mother's joke.

Lila joins in weakly, against her better judgment.

MOTHER (CONT'D)
(to Lila)
Don't you agree, dear?

Lila hesitates.

NATHAN
Of course she does, mother.

INT. NATHAN'S BEDROOM - LATER

Nathan is in bed, in starched pajamas. He lies on his back under perfect covers and stares straight up at the ceiling.

NATHAN
I hate Wayne. Don't you?

No response.

NATHAN (CONT'D)
What are you doing in there?

LILA (O.S.)
(pissy)
I'll be out in a minute.

NATHAN
They spoil that Wayne. It's because they're elderly. They don't have the energy to be properly strict anymore. He's a holy terror.

No response.

NATHAN (CONT'D)
Listen, I'm sorry about my mother's reaction to your work. What are you doing in there?

LILA (O.S.)
You didn't seem sorry when you were laughing at her endless, stupid, cruel animal jokes.

NATHAN
I was simply attempting to keep the evening light. You know I feel similarly to you about nature.

LILA (O.S.)
Do you?

NATHAN
Of course. I love it.

Lila emerges from the bathroom, radiant, hopeful.

CONTINUED:

LILA
Do you? Oh do you, darling?

NATHAN
It's my favorite... nature.

Lila happily leaps into bed. She smothers Nathan with kisses.

LILA
Oh, I'm so relieved. Let's celebrate tomorrow with a long hike in the woods!

NATHAN
(oh shit)
That's a great idea.

Nathan kisses her.

LILA
I'll show you my old stomping grounds!

NATHAN
Terrific. Can't wait!

Nathan kisses her ear. He looks confused, sticks his finger behind her ear, and pulls it out with a dab of shaving cream.

NATHAN (CONT'D)
Shaving cream?

LILA
I don't think so.
(beat)
Why?

INT. NATHAN'S CAR - DAY

Nathan drives. He's dressed in spanking new, freshly starched safari clothes, big shiny new hiking boots. Lila sits in the front passenger seat. She is dressed in a costume identical to Nathan's, but, as opposed to Nathan, she seems awkward in it. She fidgets in it, straightens it, sighs, comes to terms with it, and looks dreamily out the window at the passing trees. She is home. That's all that matters.

NATHAN
Darling, did you bring the insect repellent lotion?

LILA
Yes, darling.

(CONTINUED)

CONTINUED:

NATHAN
Why did they need to adopt that Wayne?
(new thought)
Oh, and the sun block?

LILA
Of course.

NATHAN
What SPF, sweetie?

LILA
Forty-five.

NATHAN
Perfectomundo! We are ready!
(beat)
Say, wouldn't it be wonderful to have an insect repellent lotion that also worked as a sun block? Think of all the time one would save.

LILA
I think maybe I've seen that already.

NATHAN
No, I'm sure not. I think I'll get Johannsen in chemistry on it. Oh! Did you bring the first aid kit?

LILA
Yes. And the Flares.

NATHAN
Flares? Really? Do you think that's necessary?

LILA
Just playing.

NATHAN
(not entirely getting it)
Very good.
(then:)
y'know, my sense is that Wayne's trouble. I mean, how much do they really know about that kid? Why is he without parents in the first place?

LILA
I don't know. Maybe they died.

CONTINUED: (2)

NATHAN
Exactly. Exactly!

LILA
He seems nice enough, Nathan. A little quiet. You should give him a chance.

NATHAN
No, see, that's precisely what he wants. That's Wayne's little game. And I ain't playin'.
(new thought)
Hey, we could call the lotion "Quit Bugging me, Sunny."
(laughs a lot)
Get it? Sunny. S-u-n-n-y.

LILA
(laughs appreciatively)
Very funny.

NATHAN
I love you so much.

INT. CONGRESS - DAY

Puff testifies.

PUFF
Then, gentlemen, one day I saw something I hadn't seen since my father's death. I saw other apes. They chattered away in what seemed to be gibberish. Later I learned it was English. Now I wonder if perhaps my initial assessment hadn't been correct.

DISSOLVE TO:

EXT. FOREST - DAY

Puff's POV: Through some brush we watch Nathan and Lila hiking. We hear Puff's loud heavy breathing and, in the distance, the relentless gibberish chatter of Nathan and Lila. Puff moves. Lila glances over.

INTERROGATION ROOM - NIGHT

Lila talks.

LILA
I saw a flash of white.

EXT. FOREST - DAY

We're with Lila and Nathan now. Lila has stopped and is peering into the distance.

LILA
Did you see that?

NATHAN
What?

LILA
I don't know. Something.

NATHAN
A deer?

LILA
Too... upright. A person?

NATHAN
(nervously)
It might behoove us to turn back at this point.

Lila walks in the direction of the sighting.

NATHAN (CONT'D)
(not budging)
If it's a person, why should we go see it? It's not like it's nature.
(beat, calling after)
Lila, people who live in the woods don't want to be seen. We have to respect their wishes. Lila trudges through the brush. Nathan follows. Better than being left behind.

NATHAN (CONT'D)
This is the way to get ticks, Lila. This is it. Bingo! Lyme Disease! You've hit the nail on the head here. Lila is in her element. Her whole demeanor has changed. She is tracking. She sniffs the breeze, cocks her head, moves stealthily. Then she sheds her clothes, almost shaking them off, like a dog shaking off some cute costume his owner had dressed him in.

NATHAN (CONTÍD)
Oh for God's sa --

(CONTINUED)

CONTINUED:

Lila turns her head and glares at Nathan. There is an animal fierceness in her eye that shuts him up instantly. She turns back to pursue her prey.

INT. CONGRESS - DAY

Puff testifies.

PUFF
An ape as I had never seen before.

DISSOLVE TO:

EXT. FOREST - DAY

Puff's POV: We see a naked Lila looking in our general direction, but not seeing us. The sun dapples her body. She moves closer and closer.

PUFF
Like me, yet different. And all at once I felt a heat pass through me. Gentlemen, I wanted to touch her, caress her, to be one with her. I had urges I could not explain. So I did what any animal would do in that situation...

INT. INTERROGATION ROOM - NIGHT

The cops are transfixed.

LILA
He bolted.

EXT. FOREST - DAY

We are with Lila. She creeps along, when suddenly a tan, muscular figure tears out from behind a tree and runs, practically on all fours, through the dense underbrush. Lila follows, almost as agile as the forest creature. Nathan just stands there. The chase continues. There is a great deal of heaving and panting. Puff shimmies up a large tree. Lila follows. Puff leaps from branch to branch. Lila follows easily. Puff swings from a vine. So does Lila. Finally they come to the end of the trees, a clearing. There is no nowhere for Puff to leap. Lila is with him in the tree. They are crouched, bloody, heaving, on separate branches, staring at each other. After a long moment, Lila speaks.

LILA
Who are you?

CONTINUED:

Puff cocks his head. The high timbre of her voice surprises him, pleases him, but he doesn't understand the words.

LILA (CONT'D)
You don't understand my language, do you?

Puff looks at his crotch. Apparently there is some activity down there. Lila, following his eyes, glances down there also.

LILA (CONT'D)
(laughing)
I take it back, you do understand my language.

Puff grabs for his crotch and begins to play with himself distractedly, looking at her all the while. He falls out of the tree. Lila gasps. Branches crack and snap as he passes through them, followed by an unpleasant thud as he hits the forest floor. Lila shimmies down the tree, and kneels by Puff. He is unconscious.

LILA (CONT'D)
Oh God.

Nathan comes limping through the brush. Somehow his safari suit and boots are as clean and pressed as they were in the car. He is carrying Lila's clothes, neatly folded and draped over his arm.

NATHAN
Now look what you did! Is he dead? Please put something on. Lila glances icily up at Nathan.

NATHAN (CONT'D)
You'll catch cold. It's cold.
(trying to change subject)
What do you suppose he is, a survivalist?

LILA
I think he's feral.

NATHAN
(jumping back)
Feral? Don't touch him! He could be diseased! He might ... My God, rabies!

LILA
He looks perfectly fine.

CONTINUED: (2)

NATHAN
My God, I think we should go. Please. Before he wakes and, I don't know, eats us or beats us with a stone, or whatever the feral peoples do.

LILA
I don't understand you. This is fascinating. A human being totally uncontaminated by civilization, and all you want to do is run back to your --

NATHAN
(thinking)
Hold on a minute. Hold on.

LILA
What?

NATHAN
Well, it's very, very tempting, I have to say.

LILA
Nathan, you're starting to annoy me.

NATHAN
Don't you see?
(doing a little dance)
Forget the mice! Forget guinea pigs! Forget cats, and monkeys, too. I'm on to stage five: The human subject.

LILA
Oh no.

NATHAN
(ranting)
I can change him! I can teach him. I can save this unfortunate man's life!

LILA
I won't allow you. It's wrong. He's happy here.

NATHAN
Is he, Lila? Is he happy living filthy and naked alone in this tick-infested wilderness?
(MORE)

(CONTINUED)

CONTINUED: (3)

NATHAN (CONT'D)
Never to know the love of a good woman, never to revel in the pitter-patter of little feet, never to read Moby Dick, or marvel at a Monet, or just sit back after a day of hard but rewarding work and smoke a pipe.

LILA
(weakening resolve)
You'd be taking away his freedom.

NATHAN
Freedom's just another word for nothing left to lose, Lila.

Lila looks off into the distance, her eyes brimming with tears. As Nathan continues his speech, we move closer and closer into Lila's eyes. Nathan's voice fades into nothing by the time we dissolve.

NATHAN (CONT'D)
Belonging to something, a person or a society, is a basic human craving. We are communal creatures. This poor soul has no one ...

DISSOLVE TO:

EXT. CLIFF - DUSK

A naked, hairy Lila sits alone and watches the sunset. There's a chill in the air and she shivers and hugs herself.

LILA
I have no one. God, you give me this beautiful sunset. But with no one to say, "isn't it beautiful" to, it becomes meaningless, another stupid sunset. They happen everyday. What is it that ...

DISSOLVE TO:

EXT. FOREST - DAY

Lila is hovering over the unconscious Puff. Nathan's voice comes back into focus. He is still speechifying.

NATHAN
... what is it that makes us human, if not the knowledge that we are human? Think of this deprived man's education as the greatest gift we could bestow --

(CONTINUED)

CONTINUED:

LILA
All right.

NATHAN
Great. Grab his feet. We'll throw him in the trunk.

INT. LAB - DAY

Nathan hovers over the Lucite case with the tiny dinner table in it. His assistant, Gabrielle, presses a button, a door opens, and two white mice scurry in. The male pulls out a chair for the female. The female climbs up on the chair, and the male pushes the chair in, then scurries around to the other side of the table and climbs onto his own chair. The Lucite lid over the silverware and salads lifts and both mice pick up the proper forks and begin eating. Nathan scribbles in his notebook.

GABRIELLE
Doctor ...

Nathan looks up. Gabrielle jerks her head in the direction of a very large Lucite cage. Inside, Puff, now dressed in a diaper and connected to all sorts of electrodes, is stirring. Nathan and Gabrielle hurry over.

NATHAN
Good morning.

Groggily, Puff takes in his surroundings. There's quite a lot to take in: the white room, the strange apes in strange suits, his own clothing, the wires. After surveying the scene for a moment, Puff becomes frightened and agitated. He tries to escape. Not understanding Lucite, he smashes into it, again and again. He tears at his diaper. Nathan gives a nod to Gabrielle, who presses a button on a panel. An electric shock sends Puff flying. He lies on the floor confused and dazed. After a moment, he gets up and again crashes into the Lucite. Nathan gives the signal to Gabrielle and once again she shocks Puff. He once again gets up and crashes against the Lucite. Again he is shocked. He gets up again, and is about to crash against the Lucite, but he thinks better of it, and squats in place, immobilized.

NATHAN (CONTÍD)
(to Gabrielle)
Only three shocks. A chimp takes fifteen. This is going to be tres simple, no, Gabrielle?

CONTINUED:

GABRIELLE
(in love with Nathan)
Oui, doctor, oui.

NATHAN
(to Puff)
Good morning ...
(to Gabrielle))
We need a name for him, don't we?

GABRIELLE
Oui.

NATHAN
You decide. Today is your day.

GABRIELLE
Really? My day? Well, I had a sweet little mongrel doggie named Puff when I was a girl. This one reminds me of my dog, all shaggy! So cute!
(giggles girlishly)
I loved my doggie very much, monsieur.

NATHAN
(charmed)
Puff it is then. Puff Bronfman. Is that okay?

GABRIELLE
Oui. Perfect!

NATHAN
(to Puff)
Good morning, Puff Bronfman. I'm Dr. Bronfman and this is my assistant Gabrielle. We're your mommy and daddy while you are here.

Gabrielle likes this concept a great deal. She smiles and moves closer to Nathan.

NATHAN (CONT'D)
(to Puff)
Would you like some salad, son?

Gabrielle poises her finger above the button. She winks at Nathan. He blushes.

EXT. LAB PARKING LOT - EVENING

Nathan, carrying a brief case, walks to his car. Gabrielle hurries to catch up. Her high heels click on the pavement.

(CONTINUED)

CONTINUED:

GABRIELLE
Dr. Bronfman! Dr. Bronfman!

Nathan turns.

NATHAN
Oh, hi, Gabrielle.

GABRIELLE
(out of breath)
Hi. I just wanted to tell you that I very much enjoy working with you.
(blushes)
Now I'm embarrassed that I say this.

They walk along.

NATHAN
No. Don't be. I really enjoy hearing that. You're a terrific assistant.

GABRIELLE
Merci. I ... Do you ... would you like to go get a cup of coffee, perhaps?

NATHAN
Well, I don't know. I'm actually on my way to --

GABRIELLE
Now I am truly embarrassed. Forgive me. I should not have asked such a stupid question. I know you are a very important man and --

NATHAN
No. Don't be silly.

GABRIELLE
You're so sweet.

Gabrielle stops walking and starts to cry softly. Nathan doesn't know what to do. He stops also. His eyes dart around, then.

NATHAN
There there.

Gabrielle looks up appreciatively.

GABRIELLE
You know just the right thing to say to me.

CONTINUED: (2)

She sniffs, reaches out, and holds Nathan's pinky. They both study the pinky. There is no eye-contact.

NATHAN
I hate to see you sad.

GABRIELLE
Oh, I was born sad, Doctor. Sometimes I think I could only be happy if I find a man who is strong and brave to guide me. Why are there not more men out there like you? Gabrielle looks up, into Nathan's face.

Their eyes meet.

NATHAN
I'm sure you'll find some great guy soon.

She's stung: Nathan doesn't want to be that man. She gently lets go of the pinky.

GABRIELLE
I'm so sorry. I am a foolish little thing. I am pink in the face, no? It is only that I have been so lonely lately and... I am ashamed. I'll see you tomorrow, okay? Unless... Am I fired now?

Gabrielle pouts. Nathan is charmed.

NATHAN
No, no. Of course not, Gabrielle.

GABRIELLE
I like it when you say my name. Is that stupid?

Nathan looks at her doubly charmed.

INT. NATHAN'S BEDROOM - NIGHT

Nathan, in his pajamas, lies in bed reading. He looks up.

NATHAN
What are you doing in there?

LILA (O.S.)
Nothing. Be right out.

The phone rings. Nathan picks it up.

(CONTINUED)

CONTINUED:

NATHAN
Hello?
(beat, happily)
Oh, hi, Gabrielle!

Nathan sits up in bed.

LILA (O.S.)
Who is it?

NATHAN
Uh-huh. Right, Gabrielle. Right.

Nathan laughs.

LILA (O.S.)
Who is it?

NATHAN
(into phone)
Absolutely, Gabrielle.
(covering phone, testily)
Someone from work!
(into phone)
Sorry about that, Gabrielle. Uh-huh.
Exactly.

Nathan laughs.

LILA (O.S.)
Who from work?

NATHAN
(into phone)
Excuse me one second, would you,
Gabrielle?

Nathan puts down the phone and heads to the bathroom.

LILA (O.S.)
Who is it, Nathan?

Nathan opens the bathroom door.

NATHAN
Look, Lila, when I'm on a work ...

Lila turns with a gasp. She has shaving cream all over her chest. Nathan looks stunned. He backs away.

LILA
Nathan, I ...

INT. GABRIELLE'S APT - NIGHT

The lights are low. The room is peppered with lit candles. Gabrielle, in a slip, lies on her bed, eats cherries from a bowl, and listens to Nathan and Lila's conversation on speaker.

LILA (O.S.)
It's hormonal, Nathan. I can't help it. I'm sorry.

NATHAN (O.S.)
Your entire body?

LILA (O.S.)
I'm getting electrolysis. It's working, but it takes time. So meanwhile I have to --

NATHAN (O.S.)
You have to shave? Like an ape?

LILA (O.S.)
(crying)
Apes don't shave, you son of a bitch!

NATHAN (O.S.)
Don't quibble. You know what I mean.

LILA (O.S.)
I'm sorry. Please don't be mad at me for this.

NATHAN (O.S.)
Mad? I'm... I'm ... disgusted!

LILA (O.S.)
(crying)
I'm the same person I was before you knew, damn it! Oh God!

NATHAN
I have to think! I must think!

Footsteps and a door slam. Lila is near the phone now and crying in desperate heaves.

LILA (O.S.)
Oh God, why ... do ... I ... have ... to ... be ... like -- Oh, no! Oh, shit!
(rustling sound, then into phone)
(MORE)

CONTINUED:

LILA (O.S.) (CONT'D)
Hello? Hello? Is anyone there? Who's there?

Gabrielle calmly pops another cherry in her mouth and hangs up the phone.

INT. NATHAN'S CAR - NIGHT

Nathan, in his pajamas, drives. His face is set in a furious scowl and he drives fast.

INT. GABRIELLE'S CAR - NIGHT

Gabrielle drives leisurely. She is calm, a slight smile on her face.

INT. LAB - NIGHT

Nathan paces in front of Puff's Lucite case. Puff watches suspiciously from the corner where he is huddled. The lights are off, but there is a green glow from a couple of exit signs. Nathan stops at his desk, switches on a small lamp and searches his book shelf. He pulls out a medical book, searches the index, finds the page and begins to read.

NATHAN (V.O.)
"Idiopathic hirsutism occurs in women who have hair follicles highly sensitive to normal female androgen levels. It is believed...

Nathan turns the page and comes face to face with a medical photo of a young woman suffering from this condition. It is a startling image made more startling when Nathan realizes he is looking at a younger Lila. He jumps away from the book.

NATHAN (CONT'D)
Ahhh!
(paces frantically)
I don't get it. How could I find myself in this mess? This is a mess. How do I extricate myself from it? Is my girlfriend a man? No! But she deceived me. She has hair! She's not supposed to!
(stops)
But am I being fair? So what if she has hair? I have hair.
(paces)
But I'm supposed to! I am a man. Men are supposed to have hair.
(beat)
But poor Lila. What she's had to go through.
(MORE)

(CONTINUED)

CONTINUED:

NATHAN (CONT'D)
Her courage in the face of this abomination of nature. I must love her all the more. I should love every grotesque hair on her body. She loves me and I have a mortifyingly small...

The lights flick on. Nathan turns with a start. It's Gabrielle. She's in an overcoat. She gasps.

GABRIELLE
Oh, Doctor. I did not know. I'm sorry to disturb you. I just came for some papers I left.

NATHAN
Gabrielle.
(closes the medical book)
No, I'm sorry if I startled you. I came to think.
(beat, remembering)
God, did I hang up on you?

GABRIELLE
Oui. Perhaps I called at a bad time. I am sorry.

NATHAN
No, I'm sorry. I just got distracted.

GABRIELLE
Is everything fine?

NATHAN
Oui.
(laughs)
Now you've got me talking French.

GABRIELLE
(laughs)
I was in my p.j.'s when I remembered I left some papers I need to go over.
(opens overcoat to reveal lingerie)
See? I rushed right out of the house. I must look a mess. I'm so embarrassed

NATHAN
(taken)
No. Not at all.

Puff is taken also. His eyes are wide.

NATHAN (CONT'D)
I'm in my p.j.'s, too. Funny, huh?

GABRIELLE
A coincidence, yes?
(beat)
And how is our son?

NATHAN
Our ...? Oh!
(laughs, out of control)
He seems fine. I guess we woke him. The lights and all.

GABRIELLE
I should turn them off.
(she does)
Maybe I sing him a lullaby my mama sang to me when I was a little girl.

NATHAN
(a little giddy)
When you were a little French girl?

GABRIELLE
But of course, silly.

NATHAN
(trying for control)
That might be very soothing... for him... to hear... that.

Gabrielle kneels by Puff's case. Puff crawls over, tries to touch her through the Lucite. Gabrielle sings a French lullaby. It's very sweet. Nathan watches her, looks at her thigh, her hair, the delicate way the tip of her nose moves when she sings.

GABRIELLE
(singing)
Fay doh doh lolo anty frar/Fay doh doh tohah day kolah/Mamo ah toh key fay doo gah-toe/Papa ay tobah fay doo chocolah
Puff gets drowsy.

He curls up on the floor and sleeps.

GABRIELLE (CONT'D)
(quietly to Nathan)
There.

Nathan stares at her, transfixed. She pretends not to notice.

GABRIELLE (CONT'D)
Shall we close up then?

NATHAN
Maybe we should just sit for a while.
It's very peaceful.

GABRIELLE
It's nice, yes. I'm glad I ran into you,
both in our silly pajamas. It is two
happy coincidences, no?

NATHAN
Yes. Happy happy.

GABRIELLE
Yet you look so sad. A great man like
you should never ever have to be sad.

NATHAN
I'm fine. Life is funny, that's all.

Gabrielle stands. She stretches languorously, revealing a
lot of leg.

GABRIELLE
Now I am sleepy, too. Soooo sleepy.

NATHAN
I shouldn't say this, but you're pretty,
Gabrielle. It's unprofessional, I know.

GABRIELLE
Really? I always think myself so ugly.
No, not ugly, but plain. A wallflower.

NATHAN
(buying her line)
Really? No. Not at all. You're a very
pretty girl. You should know that. You
should be confident.

GABRIELLE
Thank you so much. Merci. It is too
wonderful to hear a man say such a nice
compliment.

NATHAN
It's true. I wouldn't lie.

GABRIELLE
You are sweet to me.

Gabrielle walks slowly by Nathan. He inhales deeply,
breathing her in. She smiles to herself. He reaches out
touches her leg.

CONTINUED: (4)

GABRIELLE (CONT'D)
(vaguely protesting)
Doctor.

She moves into Nathan. She presses her thigh against his shoulder. Nathan leans forward, kisses her exposed thigh.

NATHAN
So soft. So smooth.
(back to reality)
I'm sorry. It's just ...

GABRIELLE
(soothing)
Shh.

INT. NATHAN'S BATHROOM - NIGHT

Lila is shaving herself all over. Shaving and weeping. There are nicks all over her body. She has no eyebrows any more. The hair on her head is hacked off.

INT. LAB - NIGHT

Nathan and Gabrielle are lying naked on the floor. Gabrielle rests her head on Nathan's chest.

NATHAN
Was that okay? I mean, was I able to ... satisfy you?

GABRIELLE
You are like an animal, I think. Tres erotique to me.

NATHAN
Really? Wow! That's that's terrific to hear from someone so ... feminine, so female.

GABRIELLE
I love being female because, how do you say, it allows me to be close to men.

NATHAN
(crazily)
I love you being female, too.
(beat)
Do you think our boy witnessed the primal scene? They look over at the case.

Puff's eyes are closed.

CONTINUED:

GABRIELLE
(shrugs and laughs)
Anyway, even if he did, it's time he grew up. N'est-ce pas?
(sighs, runs her fingers along his chest)
Oh, goodness, I love chest hair on a man. I know it isn't fashionable now, the hairy man. But to me it is the very sign of masculinity. To be hairless on the chest, that is for the woman to be. Don't you think so?

Nathan tenses. Gabrielle looks up innocently at him.

GABRIELLE (CONT'D)
What is wrong, my darling?

NATHAN
Nothing, my darling. All is right.

Gabrielle smiles to herself.

INT. CONGRESS - DAY

Puff testifies.

PUFF
I saw it, gentlemen. I saw the whole sweaty, passionate, ugly, beautiful act, and to use the vernacular, I wanted me some of that.

The congressmen laugh appreciatively. The laughter is a little too enthusiastic and goes on a little too long. It peters out.

PUFF (CONT'D)
And I think I understood from that moment, that in order to get some, I would have to play their game.

The congressmen nod sadly, in recognition of this reality.

INT. LAB - DAY

Puff, in his Lucite case, sits behind a set dinner table. He seems attentive, calm, interested as Nathan teaches him table manners. Gabrielle stands very close, almost possessively close, to Nathan. She wears a lab coat, but it is unbuttoned, and underneath she is wearing a skin-tight black minidress. She strokes the back of Nathan's head as he works with Puff.

(CONTINUED)

CONTINUED:

NATHAN
(slow. Talking to an idiot)
Excellent, Puff. Now, the lady you're with excuses herself to go powder her nose. The wheels turn in Puff's head. He thinks hard. Then he stands. Gabrielle shrieks and claps happily.

NATHAN (CONT'D)
Perfect. Perfect, Puff!

Nathan leans over and kisses Gabrielle. Puff watches. He makes an exaggerated kissy-face, pursing his lips, trying to imitate Nathan. The phone rings. Gabrielle pulls herself away and, giggling as Nathan tries to keep her from going, picks up the phone.

GABRIELLE
Dr. Bronfman's line. Yes. One moment please.
(puts it on hold)
Lila.

NATHAN
Shit.
(takes phone)
Hi, honey.

INT. NATHAN'S LIVING ROOM - NIGHT

Lila sits on the couch. Eyebrows are attractively drawn onto her face. She wears a very femme blonde wig. Lots of make-up.

LILA
So, how's it going today?

NATHAN (O.S.)
Good. Making progress.

LILA
Honey, can we talk tonight? You know, about stuff? Things have been so strained for the past few weeks, since you know, and I just want to talk.

INT. LAB - NIGHT

Nathan, phone cradled between shoulder and ear, puts his face in his hand. Gabrielle rests a hand on his shoulder.

CONTINUED:

NATHAN
Everything's fine. We don't need to talk. Besides I have to work late.

LILA (O.S.)
Please, Nathan. I really need this. You've been working late a lot.

Nathan looks up helplessly at Gabrielle.

NATHAN
Okay, we'll have dinner tonight.

Gabrielle gets mad, exhales sharply, pulls her hand away. Nathan gives her a pleading look, grabs for her. She moves away.

NATHAN (CONT'D)
Yeah. Okay. Be home around seven. Okay, bye.
(hangs up)
What? I'm sorry. What was I supposed to do?

GABRIELLE
(disgusted)
I don't know, Nathan. What are you supposed to do?

NATHAN
You don't abandon somebody because they have a physical problem.

GABRIELLE
Funny. I thought that's exactly what you did. You just don't have the courage to admit it to yourself.

INT. WHITE SPACE - DAY

Nathan talks. A tear runs down his face, mingles with the blood.

NATHAN
I still feel guilt. Even dead. One would've hoped ... Y'know, I really did love Lila. But with her ... problem ... and then when Gabrielle revealed her feelings. She was so ... conventionally female. And she had that accent. I was lost from then on. But Gabrielle was right.
(MORE)

CONTINUED:

NATHAN (CONT'D)
I couldn't admit this shallowness of
character to myself, let alone to Lila.

INT. LIPSTICK RESTAURANT - NIGHT

Lila and Nathan eat. Lila is in her new, very feminine make-up, wig, and dress. Her table manners are impeccable, almost robotic. There is an awkward silence

LILA
Are you seeing somebody else, Nathan? I
have to know. I'm sorry to ask. But I
feel like I need to know.

NATHAN
Of course not.

LILA
It would just be helpful to know.

NATHAN
No.

LILA
Because, you know, you seem so distant.
And you work late every night. And we
hardly ever have sex, and when we do,
it's ... I don't know. It feels
different.

NATHAN
I'm just preoccupied.

LILA
'kay.
(beat)
Do you like my new look?

NATHAN
Yeah. It's nice. It's really good.

LILA
I'm trying, you know.
(starting to cry)
I'm trying to be what you want. I want
to be what you want, Nathan. All I want
is to be what you want.

NATHAN
(embarrassed)
Shh. It's okay.
(takes her hand)
You're exactly what I want.

(CONTINUED)

CONTINUED:

LILA
(hopeful, sniffing)
Really?

NATHAN
Sure. Of course.

LILA
Because I'm really trying, you know.
Louise says maybe only another two years
of electrolysis.

NATHAN
(hard to stomach)
That's great.

LILA
I've signed up for a ballet class. And
look at my nails! A real girl!

Lila holds out her hands. Her finger nails are polished fire engine red.

NATHAN
It's a great color for you.

LILA
Really? Oh, Nathan, let's have a baby!

INT. NURSERY - DAY

Lila holds and rocks a swaddled baby. She passes it to Nathan, who looks at it and sees that it's a baby monkey. Nathan shudders. Lila looks on lovingly, oblivious.

DISSOLVE TO:

INT. THERAPIST'S OFFICE - DAY

Nathan sits with his head in his hands. Wendall listens attentively.

NATHAN
So that's the nightmare I've been having.
And, for the life of me, I don't
understand it.

WENDALL
I think it may be about Lila.

NATHAN
(beat)
How? I don't --

CONTINUED:

WENDALL
Well, it seems that since Lila broached the subject of children, you've been on edge and I know you have an issue with her body hair.

NATHAN
Oh, yes, I see. Well, that's something to consider. I felt it might've been more about child-rearing concerns. The monkey-baby representing responsibility and --

WENDALL
Nathan, I think it's important for you to look at your feelings for Lila.

NATHAN
I love Lila! She's wonderful. And she loves me! That's no small potatoes. And she's a good person. How rare is that in this world? How could I stop loving someone because of a little physical imperfection, if it can even be called that?

WENDALL
And how do you feel about Gabrielle?

Nathan puts his head in his hands.

INT. LAB - DAY

Nathan is holding flash cards up to Puff. Puff tentatively reads aloud from the cards. Gabrielle sits on a stool nearby, fish-netted legs crossed, arms crossed, and an angry expression on her face.

PUFF
Good-eve-n-ing-lay-dees-and-gent-el-men.

NATHAN
Bravo, Puff! Bravo!

Puff smiles happily. Nathan and Puff both look over at Gabrielle for her approval. None is forthcoming.

NATHAN (CONT'D)
Isn't Puff doing spectacularly, honey?

GABRIELLE
Hmmmph.

CONTINUED:

NATHAN
Gabby, what is it?

GABRIELLE
Hmmph. Hmmph.
(beat)
Nathan, we have to talk, you and I.

NATHAN
Fine.

GABRIELLE
Not in front of the boy.

NATHAN
Very well.

Gabrielle stands, turns, and stomps across the room. Nathan follows her angry, switching hips with his eyes, as does Puff. She exits into the hall. Nathan looks at Puff and shrugs. Puff returns the shrug. Nathan follows Gabrielle into the hall.

INT. LAB HALLWAY - DAY

Gabrielle stands there waiting, a troubled look on her face, her eyes brimming. Nathan emerges, tries to embrace her.

NATHAN
My little French girl.

GABRIELLE
(pushing him away)
Stop. Get away.

NATHAN
What is it?

GABRIELLE
You have to choose, Nathan. It's like Sophie's choice. Only it is Nathan's choice. Did you ever see that movie, Sophie's Choice? It is like that. Only it is this.

NATHAN
Gab, you know I'm trying to sort things out.

GABRIELLE
(hard)
No! It is now that you must decide.
(soft)
(MORE)

(CONTINUED)

CONTINUED:

GABRIELLE (CONT'D)
I love you, Doctor Nathan ...
(hard)
... but I will not wait. I will not be your chippy, your little Mademoiselle Parlez-vous side dish.
(soft)
I want to have a sweet tiny baby inside my belly ... from you.

Nathan gets a faraway look in his eyes.

DISSOLVE TO:

EXT. BEACH - DAY

Nathan and Gabrielle sit on a blanket on this otherwise empty beach. There is a light breeze. Gabrielle has one of her breasts exposed and is nursing an infant. Nathan looks at the baby's face. It is angelic. He looks up and smiles at Gabrielle. She smiles back. They kiss.

DISSOLVE TO:

INT. LAB HALLWAY - DAY

Nathan snaps out of his reverie, looks pleadingly at the waiting Gabrielle.

NATHAN
I love you so much, Gabrielle ...

GABRIELLE
But? ... But? There's a "but", Nathan.

NATHAN
I don't know how to leave Lila.

Gabrielle tears off her lab coat. Underneath she is wearing practically nothing, a skimpy black dress. She throws the lab coat at Nathan, turns and storms down the hall. Nathan watches her until she disappears around the corner. He brings the lab coat up to his face and breathes in her fragrance.

INT. NATHAN'S APT - NIGHT

Lila, all prettied up and civilized and manicured, is setting the table for dinner. She is humming. Nathan walks in the door. Lila doesn't hear him. He stands in the doorway for a moment, watching Lila from behind. His face is blank. Lila catches sight of him. She's startled.

(CONTINUED)

human nature

I'm not sorry. So I spend the rest of my life in jail.

I've been in jail my whole life anyway.

A jail of blood and tissue and coursing

hormones. . . A jail called the human body.

I am sorry, gentlemen, sorry for all of us.

Yours is a complicated, sad world. I was living

a life of simplicity when I was ripped from

my Eden and immersed in this harshness.

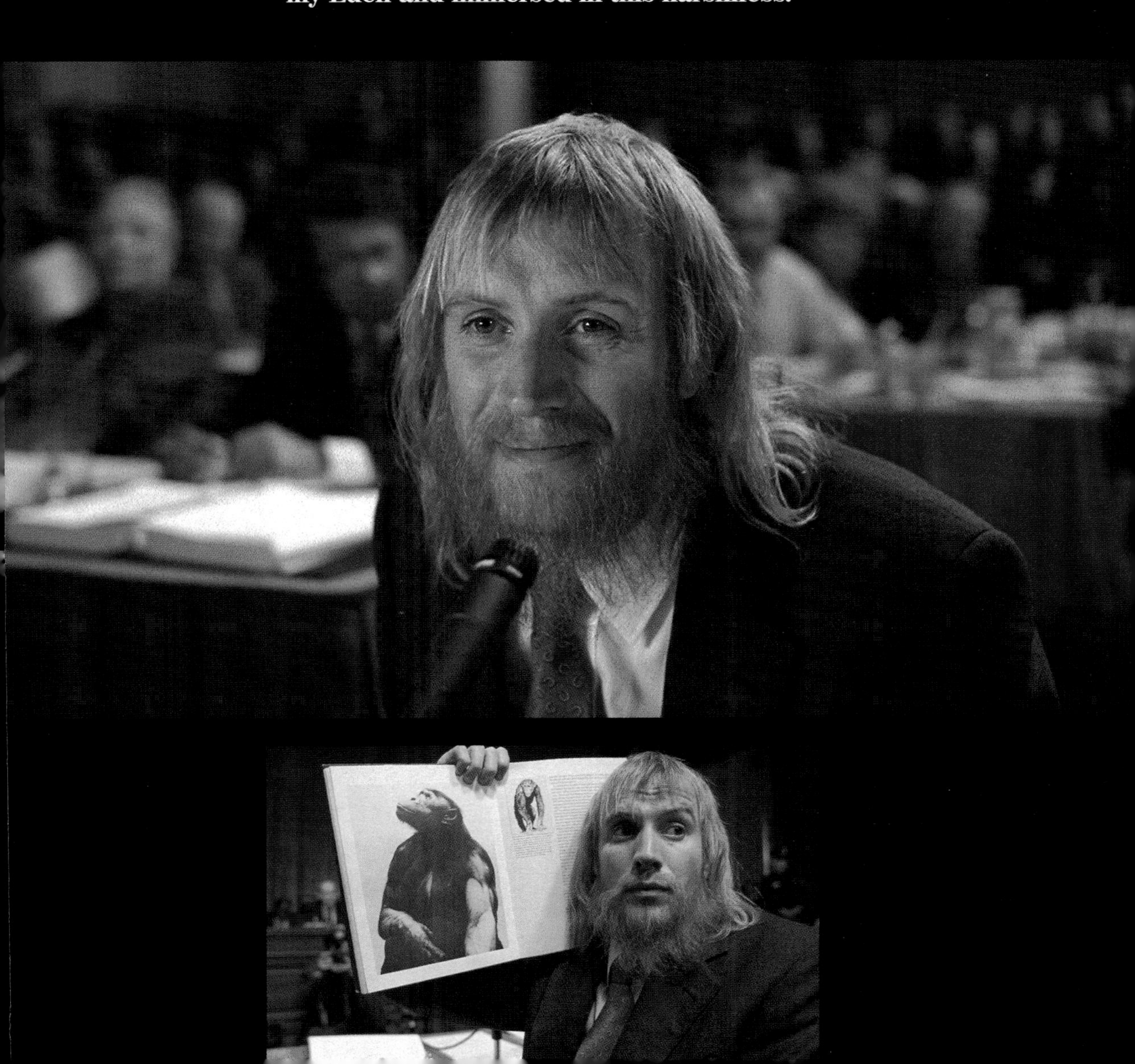

but here sorry is meaningless. Love is meaningless. Jealousy is meaningless.

I don't even know what sorry means anymore. It's odd. When I was alive I knew—maybe it was all I knew—

. . . I guess that's how I can be sure I'm really dead.

Until a national tragedy undid all those years of therapy

and reminded him what the human race was truly about.

So your part of the bargain is to never wallow in the filth of instinct. Any dumb animal can do that.

QUEEN
KONG

and the cuddly ol' bear/
I used to be embarrassed/
of hair not fit to caress/
Now I'm so sure it's a blessing/
I've got no need of dressing

My new friends/
These split ends/
Far away from those terrible stares
The squirrels don't mind/
Nor do ravens/

I once thought God/
a creator diabolical/
He gave the nod/
To each one of my follicles/
head to my baby toe

If a girl is furred or clean shaven/
Creatures are kind/
So I have found my new green haven/
And I ain't gonna go/
Cause I'm one of them, you know.

Courtesy, decorum, manners, are all sadly lacking from our daily intercourse. Rudeness, vulgarity, meanness are the norm. . . . Ergo if I can teach table manners to mice, I can teach them to humans. If I can teach table manners to humans, maybe I can make this world a little bit safer.

Good morning, Puff Bronfman. I'm Dr. Bronfman and this is my assistant Gabrielle. We're your mommy and daddy while you are here. Would you like some salad, son?

I saw it, gentlemen. I saw the whole sweaty, passionate, ugly, beautiful act, and to use the vernacular, I wanted me some of that. . . . And I think I understood from that moment, that in order to get some, I would have to play their game.

CHALFON
5

CONTINUED:

LILA
Oh!
(laughs)
I didn't see you there, sneaky boy!
(runs over and kisses him)
You're like a boy sneaking in ...

NATHAN
(so bored)
... the back door of a movie theater.
Yes, indeed.

LILA
You remember that line from my first
book? I'm so touched!
(kisses him again)
What's wrong?

NATHAN
Nothing. Hard day. Gonna have a drink.

LILA
I'll make it.
(beats him to the portable bar)
I'm so happy, Nathan! Everything's going
to be great! Scotch on the rocks, right?
(giggles)
Just kidding. I know what you drink,
mister. I know what you drink.
(pours and blends and shakes,
etc.)
Voila!

Lila hands Nathan a frothy pink concoction with a pineapple wedge sticking out of it.

NATHAN
Thanks.

Nathan stares contemplatively out the window and sips his drink. Lila watches him, comes up behind him, puts her arms around him. Nathan cringes, but tries to cover it. Lila feels the cringe, but pretends not to have. She keeps her arms around him for a moment longer, then casually removes them.

LILA
(fishing)
How's work?

NATHAN
Cruddy, okay? Are you satisfied?

LILA
(pouty)
I don't want your work to be cruddy.

NATHAN
My assistant quit today. Okay? He was highly valuable to the project.

LILA
Oh, baby. I'm sorry. Can't you hire somebody else?

NATHAN
I guess. Whatever.

Lila screws up her face in concentration, trying to come with a viable solution to Nathan's problem.

LILA
Hey! I could come work for you! I know I haven't been all that supportive of this project, but I've come around.

NATHAN
Have you?

LILA
Oh yes, baby! I think it's a wonderful project, taking this poor uncivilized creature and turning him into a human being! What a wonderful, compassionate man you are!

NATHAN
Really?

LILA
Yes! And I want to help. I was thinking of giving up that crazy nature writing anyway.

NATHAN
How come?

LILA
Who needs it? I have you and I have being a woman and I have thinking about womanly things! I love being female because --

NATHAN
Such as what womanly things?

LILA
Such as knowing my man and how to please him!
(kisses him)
Such as making wonderful dinners for my man!
(kisses him again, leads him to the table, sits him down)
Such as looking pretty for my man!

INT. INTERROGATION ROOM- NIGHT

LILA
I had sold my fucking soul.

INT. WHITE SPACE - DAY

NATHAN
I let her sell her soul. I stood by as she did it. It's inexcusable.
(beat)
At the time though I thought it might be good for her.

INT. CONGRESS - DAY

PUFF
When she came to work with Nathan, she seemed different, gentlemen, I don't know, somehow soulless.

INT. LAB - DAY

Puff is in his case in formal evening wear in a makeshift opera box. There is a mannequin woman sitting next to him and a boom box pumping out Beethoven's Fidelio. Puff seems attentive, refined, occasionally bringing a pair of opera glasses up to his eyes, pinky extended. Outside the case, Nathan and Lila look on. The opera is over. Puff stands, applauds, yells "Bravo", and tosses a rose in the direction of the imaginary stage. The rose hits the Lucite wall and falls to the floor. Nathan and Lila stand and applaud Puff.

NATHAN
Bravo to you, Puff!

LILA
That was wonderful!

Puff smiles and performs a foppish bow, almost a curtsy. He picks up the rose, sniffs it, dramatically savoring its scent.

INT. ROMANTIC ROOM - NIGHT

Nathan and Gabrielle are having sex in a room glowing with candle light. The sex is focused and intent, although Gabrielle keeps chattering away in her delightfully cute accent.

GABRIELLE
You were wonderful today, darling. Such authority with the ape-man boy. It made me so hot for you.

NATHAN
Unnhh.

GABRIELLE
The way you are taming him. It sends chills down my girlish spine and ... everywhere else, too.

NATHAN
Urgh.

GABRIELLE
Tame me, darling! Tame your little monkey of love!

There is a mutual climax. A moment of silence, then a spent Nathan rolls off onto his side of the bed.

INT. NATHAN'S BEDROOM - NIGHT

As Nathan rolls over, we see that it is really Lila in bed with him, not Gabrielle.

LILA
(sighing)
Well, I'm tamed, Dr. Bronfman.

Nathan stares up at the ceiling.

NATHAN
I'm glad ... my assistant.

INT. LAB - DAY MONTAGE

We see a montage of interactions between Nathan, Puff, and Lila. Nathan demonstrates the proper way to taste wine: sniffing the cork, swishing the wine around in the glass, sipping, nodding in the affirmative to the waiter. Puff, inside his case, imitates it perfectly.

INT. LAB - DAY

Nathan shows Puff a flashcard which reads: "I'll start tonight with the foie gras."

INT. LAB - DAY

Puff is holding up a small hand mirror and trimming nose hairs. Lila applauds.

INT. LAB - DAY

Puff juggles three balls while riding a unicycle.

INT. LAB - DAY

Puff, dressed as Peter Pan, stands with legs spread and hands on hips. He is singing "I Gotta Crow."

INT. LAB - DAY

Puff, dressed, in an apron and chef's hat, is tossing a salad. There are two types of vinegar to choose from. He hesitates, then chooses the balsamic. Nathan and Lila applaud.

INT. LAB - DAY

Puff, in a smoking jacket and smoking a pipe, is sitting in an easy chair, next to a fake fire and a fake sleeping dog, and reading a book of poems by Yeats. Lila and Nathan, outside the case, applaud and embrace.

END MONTAGE

INT. LAB - DAY

NATHAN
I think he's ready.

LILA
Oh boy!

PUFF
(jumping up)
Oh boy!

NATHAN
Now, Puff, we're leaving on the electric collar. I don't think we'll need to shock you, but just in case.

(CONTINUED)

CONTINUED:

PUFF
Okay. That's fair.

Nathan unlocks the case. Puff tentatively steps out into the world. He hugs Nathan. It's a grateful, obsequious, slightly pathetic hug. Nathan hugs him back, but he's keeping him at a distance. Puff pulls himself out of the hug, but still rests his hands on Nathan's shoulders and looks him in the eye, almost like a lover. Then he parts with Nathan, and goes over to embrace Lila. She graciously receives him. After a moment in the embrace, Puff starts dry-humping Lila. Lila can't get out of his clutches.

NATHAN
No, Puff! Bad.

Nathan presses a button, which shocks Puff and sends him flying. Puff appears disoriented, then gets up off the floor, brushes himself off, and turns to Lila with a bow of his head.

PUFF
My apologies, madam.

LILA
It's okay, Puff.

PUFF
Shan't happen again.

EXT. BIG CITY STREET - DAY

Lila, Nathan, and Puff walk along. Puff is astounded by everything he sees. He looks with wonderment at the tall buildings, the cars, the many different types of people. He looks like an idiot.

INT. FANCY RESTAURANT - DAY

Puff, Lila, and Nathan are eating lunch. Everything is very proper. Puff is doing wonderfully.

NATHAN
This is great, Puff. You're doing fine.

PUFF
I'm loving this. It's such a treat to be out and about. What a wonderful invention a city is.

tThe immense buildings of glass and steel glinting in the afternoon sun, the smartly dressed women in their best summer frocks, the colorful street vendors. The waitress comes by.

CONTINUED:

WAITRESS
How is everything?

PUFF
Just spectacular. Great salmon.
Fantastico! You've got to give me the
recipe! My compliments to the chef!

WAITRESS
I'm glad you --

Puff stands, grabs her and starts humping her.

NATHAN
Puff, no!

Nathan presses a button on a small black box. Puff falls to the floor. The waitress looks on, sort of confused.

WAITRESS
So will that be all?

INT. TAXI - DAY

Lila, Nathan, and Puff are in the back seat of the moving taxi.

PUFF
It shan't happen again. I swear it. I'm
just getting my sea legs, you know.

LILA
(patting Puff on the back)
It's an animal urge, Puff. It's nothing
to be ashamed of.

NATHAN
Lila! Tell him.

Lila looks at Nathan, amends her statement.

LILA
(to Puff)
You just have to control it. We're not
monkeys.

NATHAN
Thank you very much for that.

INT. LAB - DAY

Puff sits in a chair and faces a screen, the collar around his neck. Nathan and Lila stand behind him at a slide projector.

PUFF
I don't think aversion therapy is really necessary, doctor. I understand the problem.

NATHAN
Humor me, Puff. It's essential that I am able to trust you out in the world.

PUFF
I bow to your expertise in these matters.

NATHAN
Lila?

Lila dims the lights and switches on the projector. An image of a pretty, fully clothed woman appears on the screen. Puff's eyes widen, but he remains seated.

NATHAN (CONT'D)
Good. You're doing fine.

The slide changes to a naked woman standing in a neutral position, no expression on her face. Puff twitches, but stays seated.

NATHAN (CONT'D)
Excellent.

The slide changes to another photo of the same woman in the same position, but with a seductive smile on her face. Puff clutches the arms of the chairs.

NATHAN (CONT'D)
You're doing very nicely, Puff. I'm pleased.

The slide changes to another picture of the same women, this time she is naked, has her back to the camera, is sticking her ass out, and looking over her shoulder at the viewer with shiny, heavily lipsticked, pursed lips. Puff is shaking.

NATHAN (CONT'D)
Great ...

Puff leaps screaming from his chair and lunges for the screen. Nathan grabs the box and jolts him.

(CONTINUED)

CONTINUED:

Puff goes flying in the air and lands with a crack. He heaves for a while, then leaps up and runs for the screen again. Again Nathan shocks him. Again he lands on the floor. He heaves, stands, lunges for the screen. Nathan shocks him. This happens seven more times. Smoke is pouring from the collar. Puff struggles to his feet. He looks at the screen.

PUFF
(shrugging, unimpressed)
Eh.

Puff sits down in his chair, and studies his finger nails. Nathan switches off the projector.

NATHAN
Excellent work, Puff. Extra dessert tonight.

PUFF
Yahoo!

NATHAN
Tomorrow, the acid test.

INT. CHESTER'S RESTAURANT - DAY

This is a Hooters-type establishment called "Chester's." The waitresses are very busty and in tight T-shirts which are emblazoned with the name of the restaurant. Lila, Nathan, and Puff sit at a table. Puff studies his menu intently, not daring to look up. Lila looks around uncomfortably. A waitress approaches.

CHESTER'S WAITRESS
How y'all doin' today?

NATHAN
(cheerily)
Very well.

LILA
(awkwardly)
Very well.

PUFF
(looking down)
Very well.

CHESTER'S WAITRESS
Good enough! What can I get for you?

NATHAN
Puff, why don't you order first?

(CONTINUED)

CONTINUED:

PUFF
(looking at menu)
Uh, what's a Rueben, please?

The waitress leans over to study the menu. Her breasts are in Puff's face.

CHESTER'S WAITRESS
What's a what, sweetheart? Oh, the Rueben? That's a sandwich with corned beef and sauer ...

PUFF
Fine. That's what I'll have. Corned beef is a good, decent meat and... Someone else please go now please.

INT. LAB HALLWAY - DAY

Lila, Nathan, and Puff walk along.

NATHAN
Puff, I'm proud of you! You did remarkably well under difficult circumstances.

LILA
Absolutely!

Puff jumps up and down excitedly.

PUFF
Did I? I tried so hard! I really concentrated! Oh, I'm so happy!

NATHAN
And because you did so well, we have a little surprise for you.

PUFF
(happily)
Extra dessert?

NATHAN
Even better.

INT. LAB - DAY

Lila, Nathan, and Puff enter. Puff sees his Lucite case. It has been transformed into a bachelor pad. Inside is a king-size bed, a TV, a couch, coffee table, shelves lined with books, a small kitchenette. There is a curtain which can be drawn for privacy. Puff is taken aback.

NATHAN AND LILA

Surprise! Puff gasps and runs into the room. He is thrilled. Nathan holds up a key.

NATHAN
Free to come and go as you please. There's some "mad money" in the night table drawer.

PUFF
(taking the key, hugging Nathan)
It's wonderful! Do you think I'm ready? Do you really?

NATHAN
I trust you'll make good, mature decisions. I trust you'll do the proper thing. Puff looks to Lila, who smiles at him broadly and nods enthusiastically.

Puff turns back to Nathan.

PUFF
Oh, I will!
(gravely)
Your very trust has instilled an enormous sense of responsibility in me. I don't want to disappoint you.

NATHAN
Good. Remember, when in doubt: Don't ever do what you really want to do.

LILA
(with no irony)
That's the key.

PUFF
(taking it in)
Got it.

INT. NATHAN'S LIVING ROOM - NIGHT

Lila and Nathan sit as far as possible from each other and read books. Nathan looks at his watch.

INT. PUFF'S LUCITE CASE - NIGHT

Puff, dressed identically to Nathan, reads Moby Dick and smokes a pipe.

(CONTINUED)

CONTINUED:

He distractedly taps his foot, stands and studies a Monet print on his wall. His foot is still nervously tapping. He checks his watch.

INT. NATHAN'S LIVING ROOM - NIGHT

Nathan stands.

NATHAN
I'm going to go down and check on Puff. See how he's holding up.

LILA
(stretching)
Should I come with?

NATHAN
Nah. You just relax. How's the book?

LILA
(lazily, happy)
Mmmm. It's good.

Nathan kisses Lila on the forehead.

NATHAN
I won't be long.

INT. NATHAN'S CAR - NIGHT

Nathan drives with a determined look on his face.

INT. GABRIELLE'S APARTMENT - NIGHT

The apartment is a mess. Every single light is on. Gabrielle is lounging in a stained nightshirt with a dopey cartoon bear on the front. She's got some sort of pimple medication dabbed on her face. She unconsciously but ferociously bites her nails as she watches TV and talks on the phone. There is no trace of a French accent.

GABRIELLE
(into phone)
You're kidding! Holy shit.
(beat)
No, duh! I had a wild hair up my ass over that for a month. Look, I'm not gonna let some Dick waltz back into my life twenty years after just 'cause he happens to be the shmuck who knocked up my goddamn mother. I mean --

There's a knock at the door.

(CONTINUED)

CONTINUED:

GABRIELLE (CONT'D)
Yeah? What?

NATHAN (O.S.)
Hi. It's Nathan.

Gabrielle's eyes widen. She jumps up from the couch and starts straightening.

GABRIELLE
(into phone)
Call you back.
(hangs up, assumes French accent)
You bastard! What do you want?

NATHAN (O.S.)
I just want to talk.

GABRIELLE
(ripping off her nightshirt)
We have nothing to say! You are a rotten bastard, that's what!

INT. GABRIELLE'S HALLWAY - NIGHT

Nathan stands there leaning against the door.

NATHAN
Please. Just one minute of your time.

GABRIELLE (O.S.)
Why? You've made your decision, Mister Stinky American. Now I hate you! No, I don't hate you; I don't even think about you!

NATHAN
I've got some things to tell you.

INT. GABRIELLE'S APARTMENT - NIGHT

Gabrielle is standing in front of a mirror, holding different sexy outfits up to herself, trying to decide.

GABRIELLE
Like what?

NATHAN (O.S.)
Well, I think it would be easier if I could talk to you face to face.

(CONTINUED)

CONTINUED:

GABRIELLE
What for?

INT. GABRIELLE'S HALLWAY - NIGHT

We hear banging and rustling and arranging coming from inside the apartment.

NATHAN
Well, I think ...

GABRIELLE (O.S.)
You think too much. I need a man who doesn't think so much but acts more than he thinks ... is what I need!

NATHAN
What?

GABRIELLE
You heard me! You make me sick when you pretend to not understand what I am saying to you! Go away from here!

NATHAN
(turning away)
Well, look, I'm sorry to have bothered you.

He starts to head down the hall.

GABRIELLE (O.S.)
(beat, then screaming)
All right, already! Come in if you must! The door's open, you son of a bitch!
Nathan heads back to the apartment, tries the knob. The door's open. He enters.

INT. GABRIELLE'S APARTMENT - NIGHT

The lights are low. The place is neat. Cool jazz plays quietly in the background. Candles are lit. Gabrielle is nowhere to be found. Nathan takes it all in. It's quite seductive.

GABRIELLE (O.S.)
In here, you lousy piece of merde.

Nathan follows her voice. He exits into the bedroom.

INT. GABRIELLE'S BEDROOM - NIGHT

Candles in here also. Gabrielle, now made up and in a satin teddy, lounges in bed, eating cherries from a bowl. Nathan just stares. She is slightly out of breath, but trying to conceal it. A film of perspiration glistens on her brow.

GABRIELLE
(testy)
Well?

NATHAN
God, you're beautiful.

GABRIELLE
Please. I look a mess.

NATHAN
No. You look so beautiful.

GABRIELLE
Anyway. Come already to the point.

NATHAN
I'm ... I'm going to leave Lila. I can't stop thinking about you.

GABRIELLE
I've moved on.

NATHAN
No!

GABRIELLE
I've been seeing Johannsen in chemistry.

NATHAN
(raging)
That goddamn Neanderthal? I'm the one who gave him the idea for the combination bug spray-sun screen! Did you know that?!

GABRIELLE
(calm, dismissive)
That's not how he tells it.

NATHAN
Of course not, that Swedish thief! He's a thief of hearts!
(beat)
I love you, Gabrielle.

CONTINUED:

GABRIELLE
(dismissive)
Hunh.

NATHAN
Just give me some time to let Lila down easily. She's a really nice girl and I don't want to hurt her more than is necessary.

GABRIELLE
(beat)
You hurt me, you know, when you made Nathan's Choice. Does that not even matter to you, you pig?

Gabrielle cries quietly. Nathan moves closer to her. He strokes her hair.

NATHAN
Can you ever forgive me?

Gabrielle looks up at him. Her expression is noncommittal and pouty, but she grabs his arm and pulls him down on top of her.

INT. STRIP CLUB - NIGHT

Puff, dressed a bit like a Victorian dandy, sits in the front row and watches a naked woman on stage dancing. A topless cocktail waitress comes by with a fresh drink for him. She takes away his empty glass. He is horribly drunk and holding himself with exaggerated rigidity -- an amateur drinker's attempt to look sober.

INT. NATHAN'S APT - NIGHT

Nathan enters. Lila sits on the couch still reading. She looks up.

NATHAN
Hey.

Nathan kisses her on the forehead.

LILA
You were gone a long time.

NATHAN
(sits down next to her)
Yeah. Puff and I got into a big, philosophical discussion.
(MORE)

CONTINUED:

NATHAN (CONT'D)
He's really quite well read, considering he's only been literate for a month now. He's going to make us famous, Lila.

LILA
So he's doing okay?

NATHAN
Seemed fine. Quiet evening enjoying his new digs.

LILA
That's funny because, y'know, I just went and picked him up at some flophouse on the lower eastside. He called here when he ran out of his "mad" money after spending an entire evening drinking, watching strippers, and fucking a whore!
(then casually)
Oh, And what did you do tonight, honey?

NATHAN
Shit.

LILA
And what did you do tonight, honey?

NATHAN
I've fallen in love with somebody else, Lila.

LILA
(pointedly)
And what did you do tonight, honey?

NATHAN
I fucked her! Okay? I fucked her. I'm sorry. But that's what the hell I did.

LILA
(standing)
Do you know what I gave up to be with you?

NATHAN
Yes.

LILA
I gave up my soul, my beliefs. I gave up my body hair!

NATHAN
Yeah, well, I'm sorry. The human heart is a strange thing.

CONTINUED: (2)

LILA
What the hell would you know about the human heart?

NATHAN
(moving to her)
Lila ...

Lila turns around and slugs him, square on the jaw, hard, knocking him to the floor.

LILA
How's that for ladylike, Nathan.

Lila opens up the hall closet and pulls out a suitcase.

INT. INTERROGATION ROOM - NIGHT

Lila looks pale and shaken. She smokes.

LILA
For two weeks I holed myself up in a motel room. I didn't even know who I was. My world had crumbled. There is nothing that makes you feel dirtier than finally deciding to sell your soul and finding no buyers.

INT. LILA'S MOTEL ROOM - DAY

Lila lies in bed watching TV. The curtains are drawn. She is a mess. The room is a mess. The wig is off. There's hair sprouting on her face. There's a knock at the door.

LILA
No maid service! For God's sake, can't you read the fucking "do not disturb" sign on my fucking doorknob?

LOUISE (O.S.)
Lila, it's Louise.

LILA
(beat, quietly)
Go the fuck away, Louise. Can't you read the sign on my doorknob?

LOUISE (O.S.)
Honey, let me in.

LILA
Louise, please...

(CONTINUED)

CONTINUED:

LOUISE (O.S.)
I want to help you.

Lila gets up, drags herself to the door, and opens it. Louise stands in the doorway taking in the depressing scene.

LILA
How'd you know where I was?

LOUISE
Nathan told my brother.

LILA
Your brother should have his license revoked.

LOUISE
Yeah. That's probably true.

LILA
(suddenly crying)
Why didn't your brother tell you that Nathan was having an affair? Why didn't he tell you that, Louise? Louise holds Lila, who hangs on her as she weeps.

LOUISE
Honey, I don't know. Just because my brother's a psychologist doesn't mean he isn't full of psychology himself. That's the thing lay people never understand.

LILA
Oh, God. Oh, God.

LOUISE
Listen, come stay with me till you get your strength back. You look terrible. We'll fix you up.
(chirpy)
Free electrolysis till you're done.

Lila pulls away from Louise.

LILA
This is what I look like, Louise! This is me! I don't want to pretend anymore.

Lila climbs back into bed, pulls the covers up, sits there and looks straight ahead. Louise stands in the doorway.

CONTINUED: (2)

LOUISE
I love you, Lila. With or without hair.
Even if Nathan can't. Even if you can't.
I offer you electrolysis because that's
what I have to offer. But I want for you
whatever makes you happy. Does this?

Lila looks at the depressing hotel room. She sniffs in her snot.

LILA
(far away)
No.
(beat)
Why won't they let me be happy?
(crying)
I don't know what to do. I don't know
what to do. I don't know what to do.

LOUISE
Just something.

LILA
(finally, small and lost)
I killed Puff.

LOUISE
No, Puff's not dead.

LILA
But sort of he is. And sort of I did it.
(beat, with mounting
enthusiasm)
What if I steal Puff away, Louise? From
Nathan. What if I save Puff? Maybe
that's a way to put things right. Is it?
I think it is. Is it?

LOUISE
It sounds right. My brother says doing
something selfless for a fellow human
being is a healthy method to combat--

LILA
(crazily excited)
And you know what else? I'm gonna make
sure Nathan wants me bad when he sees me
next time. I'm going to fuck with him,
Louise. And I want him to want to fuck
me while I'm doing it.
(beat, meek)
Is that right?

(CONTINUED)

CONTINUED: (3)

LOUISE
(out of her league)
Yes. Yes it is.

INT. CONFERENCE ROOM - DAY

A bearded psychologist addresses a crowd of bearded psychologists.

BEARDED PSYCHOLOGIST
... so without further ado, I give you Dr. Nathan Bronfman and Puff.

The room bursts into applause as Nathan and Puff, in identical tuxes, walk out on stage Nathan stands behind a podium, Puff sits casually, legs crossed, in a chair.

NATHAN
Thank you. Let's get right to it. Here we have Puff the day of his capture.

A video of Puff naked in his Lucite case, clawing at it, shrieking like a banshee, and neurotically hopping up and down, is projected onto a screen behind Nathan. There is a collective gasp from the audience. Puff watches the video with amused detachment. The video stops.

NATHAN (CONT'D)
And here he is today, a scant three months later. Puff stands, bows slightly to the audience. They burst into vigorous applause.

NATHAN (CONT'D)
Puff, why don't you say a few words to the assemblage.

PUFF
It would be my pleasure, doctor.
(behind podium)
Distinguished gentlemen and ladies of the psychological community, I stand before you today, a living testament to the amazing skill of Dr. Nathan Bronfman. To say that he took me from crayons to perfume would be a vast understatement. Dr. Bronfman took me from playing with my own feces, then to crayons, and then to an appreciation of the complex works of Franz Kline, Joseph Beuys, and Marcel Duchamp. From compulsive masturbation to ...

INT. LOUISE'S APT.- MONTAGE

This sequence is Lila getting her strength back, both emotional and physical. Lila eating a good breakfast.

INT. LOUISE'S APT.

Lila struggling to do push-ups.

INT. LOUISE'S APT.

Lila studying a nature film of chimps in the wild having sex. She imitates their body movements.

INT. ELECTROLOGIST'S OFFICE - DAY

Louise performing electrolysis on Lila's face.

END MONTAGE

INT. CONFERENCE ROOM -- SIDE DOOR

Gabrielle waits in the wings.

PUFF (O.S.)
And, so, goodnight, adieu, until we meet again, au revoir.

The audience bursts into thunderous applause. Gabrielle joins in. Nathan and Puff hurry off stage. Gabrielle embraces Nathan.

GABRIELLE
You were wonderful!

NATHAN
Was I? I wasn't a tad stiff?

GABRIELLE
Don't be silly!
(hugs Puff)
And you were wonderful, too! I loved the way you said "au revoir."

Puff and Gabrielle exchange a look. She discreetly pinches Puff's butt, smiles, winks. Nathan doesn't see this. He puts his arm around Gabrielle.

NATHAN
Come on, you two. Let's go celebrate!

Nathan and Gabrielle walk on ahead. Puff lags behind, watching Gabrielle's delightful walk.

INT. CHEAP HOTEL ROOM - NIGHT

Puff sits up on his bed, looking dejected. He listens to the sounds of Nathan and Gabrielle having sex in the adjoining room. He checks his watch, gets up, gets dressed.

INT. X RATED BOOKSTORE - NIGHT

A sweaty, sick-looking Puff watches a porno film in a little booth. It ends. He steps out into the fluorescent glare of the store. He walks out past several skulking degenerates.

INT. LOUISE'S APT. -- MONTAGE

Lila doing stomach crunches.

INT. LOUISE'S APT. - DAY

Lila screaming scarily into a mirror.

INT. LOUISE'S APT. - DAY

Lila reading Rousseau

INT. ELECTROLOGIST'S OFFICE - DAY

Lila getting electrolysis on her back from Louise.

END MONTAGE

INT. LECTURE HALL - DAY

Puff is onstage demonstrating his ballroom dancing technique. He is waltzing with Gabrielle. Nathan stops the music, and picks up a microphone.

NATHAN
Now the tango.

Nathan puts a tango record on. Gabrielle and Puff perform expertly. The audience applauds.

INT. LIMO - NIGHT

Gabrielle, Nathan, and Puff are in the back. Gabrielle pours champagne.

NATHAN
I think it went swimmingly today. You two make an excellent team.

(CONTINUED)

CONTINUED:

Gabrielle's hand rests on Puff's knee as she reaches across Nathan to hand him a glass. She and Puff look at each other. Nathan is oblivious.

EXT. HOOKER STREET- NIGHT

Puff walks along checking out the prostitutes. He signals to one with a nonchalant jerk of his head.

INT. LOUISE'S APT - DAY

Lila reading the Karma Sutra.

INT. LOUISE'S APT - MONTAGE

Lila doing one-handed push-ups.

INT. LOUISE'S APT. - DAY

Lila studying a film of chimps in the wild hunting. They chase a monkey through the trees, capture it, crack open its head with their teeth and eat its brains.

INT. ELECTROLOGISTS OFFICE - DAY

Lila getting electrolysis on her stomach.

END MONTAGE

INT. AUDITORIUM - DAY

Puff addresses the crowd. Gabrielle and Nathan look on adoringly from the wings.

PUFF
To be taken from the depths of ignorance and depravity and raised to heights of refinement! This is the priceless gift bestowed upon me by Mister Dr. Nathan Bronfman.

Thunderous applause.

EXT. ALLEY - NIGHT

Puff leans against the wall drinking whiskey from a bottle, as a prostitute, down on her knees in front of him, does her business. The look on his face is not one of pleasure or even release. It is a look of decay.

INT. LOUISE'S APARTMENT - MONTAGE CONT.

Lila doing chin ups. Her sweaty, muscular arms glisten in the sun.

INT. ELECTROLOGIST'S OFFICE -- DAY

Lila getting electrolysis on her little toe. Louise moves away from her.

LOUISE
Done!

Lila stands triumphantly.

INT. LAB - DAY

Nathan and Gabrielle, in lab coats, sit chatting with Puff. Puff sneaks glances at Gabrielle's legs and cleavage. She makes his viewing possible.

GABRIELLE
(off clipboard)
So we've got seventeen new bookings, my wonderful men.

NATHAN
Terrific. We're all going to be rich and famous. Nathan kisses Gabrielle.

PUFF
Thanks to you, Nate.

NATHAN
Thanks to you, Buddy. And your diligence and intelligence. And Perseverance.

Puff blushes.

NATHAN (CONT'D)
(to Gabrielle)
And of course to you, my sweet, for your ... moral support.

PUFF
(applauding)
Here, here.

Gabrielle kisses Nathan while glancing at Puff. Frank, wearing a business suit, enters. It's guy from the freak show. In his street clothes, with his hair combed, we see he is an amazingly handsome, ideally-proportioned miniature man. He seems nervous.

(CONTINUED)

CONTINUED:

FRANK
Excuse me, are you Dr. Bronfman?

PUFF
Is that a little boy?

NATHAN
(teaching)
No, Puff. This is a midget. I guess they prefer to be called "Little People." Isn't that correct, my good man?

FRANK
In actuality I prefer to be called Dr. Edelstein.

NATHAN
Of course, my apologies. Dr. Edelstein is a fully grown adult, Puff, believe it or not, who, due to a genetic anomaly --

FRANK
Achondroplasia.

NATHAN
-- who due to achondroplasia is miniature but perfectly proportioned.
(to Frank)
Turn, please, doctor, if you would.

Frank turns.

PUFF
(jotting in notebook)
Interesting.

NATHAN
Now, Dr. Edelstein, what can we do for you?

Frank pulls out a gun. His hand shakes.

FRANK
Okay, for starters you can find your way into that ludicrous Lucite case for starters.

Nathan, Gabrielle, and Puff look frightened. They stand and back into the case.

FRANK (CONTÍD)
(to Puff)
Not you, not you!

(CONTINUED)

CONTINUED: (2)

Puff stops in his tracks.

NATHAN
(to Frank)
Look, what is this about? We have no money on these premises. Please, if you are from some little person, or rather some achondroplasiac terrorist group ...

FRANK
(cocking the gun)
I'm beginning to tire of you, Dr. Bronfman.

Nathan and Gabrielle hurry into the case. Frank closes the door behind them. Puff is frozen with fear. Lila enters. She looks different now. Savage. Strong. Sexy. She wears guerilla-like black clothing and closely hacked-off hair. She also carries a gun.

NATHAN
Lila?

LILA
Surprised, dearheart?

GABRIELLE
This is Lila?

LILA
Yeah, this is Lila, cunt. American. And proud of it.

NATHAN
Lila, you don't intend to hurt us, do you?

LILA
Eat shit, thumbtack dick!

Gabrielle starts to cry. Lila mocks her by crying with a French accent. Then she walks over to Nathan

LILA (CONT'D)
The hair's gone, Nathan. It's all taken care of. And I'm muscular now. I get looks every day on the street.

NATHAN
You're very beautiful.

LILA
So you wanna touch me, Nathan? Or what?

(CONTINUED)

CONTINUED: (3)

NATHAN
(trying to give the answer she wants)
Yes.

LILA
(walking away, pleased)
Poor baby.
(to Frank)
Thank you, Frank. You're the best.

Lila kisses Frank on the top of the head while looking at Nathan.

FRANK
Anything and everything for you, my dear.

LILA
See, Frank and I both know what it is to be shunned because of our appearance.

FRANK
"The attempt to force human beings to despise themselves... is what I call hell." Andre Malraux.

Louise enters hurriedly, carrying rope. She bends over and kisses Frank hard on the mouth for a long moment, then:

LOUISE
(to Lila)
Sorry, parking is a bitch at this place.

PUFF
(obsequious)
There's an overflow lot across the street.

LOUISE
Yeah, I found it.

Lila sees the two trained mice in the Lucite case sitting at a tiny table and very politely eating their lunch.

PUFF
Just over on Tilton. You can't miss it.

One of the mice makes eye contact with Lila.

PUFF (CONT'D)
Right next to the V.A. hospital.

DISSOLVE TO:

INT. LILA'S BATHROOM - NIGHT

Lila is naked in the bathroom and about to kill herself when she makes eye contact with the mouse on the shelf next to the tub.

DISSOLVE TO:

INT. LAB - DAY

Lila brings her focus back to the room. Everyone is watching her, waiting for some direction.

LILA
Uh, tie them up, Louise.

LOUISE
With pleasure.

Frank keeps the gun on Gabrielle and Nathan. Louise enters the case and begins to tie them up and gag them. Nathan glances at Lila. She is aware of it, but pretends not to notice. She casually stretches to show herself off. Frank studies Gabrielle. She is panicky as Louise ties her up.

FRANK
Du temps que la Nature en sa verve puissante/Concevait chaque jour des enfants monstrueux,/J'eusse aime vivre aupres d'une jeune geante,/Comme aux pieds d'une reine un chat voluptueux.

GABRIELLE
(no clue)
Oui.

EXT. LAB PARKING LOT - DAY

Puff is sitting in the car. The electric collar is back around his neck. He stares out the window at Frank, who chats with Lila and Louise. Lila holds the black control box and the Lucite case with the two mice in it.

LOUISE
I'm going to miss you.

LILA
Oh, Louise.

LOUISE
And I'm gonna miss the lifestyle having you as a client has afforded me.

(CONTINUED)

CONTINUED:

LILA
Shut up, you.

Lila laughs and hugs her.

LILA (CONT'D)
I'm so glad you two found each other.

LOUISE
Yeah.
(to Frank, suspiciously)
Hey, what were you saying to that French chick anyway?

FRANK
I was simply telling her how beautiful you are. What a lucky man I am.

LOUISE
God, you're so sexy. He's so sexy.
(kisses him)
You're a sexy liar.

LILA
I'll be in touch guys.

LOUISE
No you won't. But it's okay. You have stuff you gotta do. Lila tears up. So does Louise. They just stand there for a moment, then:

LILA
(choked)
Gotta go.

Lila hurries around the car, gets in, and drives off. Frank nestles. Louise sighs contentedly.

EXT. LILA'S CAR - DUSK

Lila's car drives along. Puff looks nervously out the window.

INT. LILA'S CAR - EVENING

Lila and Puff are driving in silence on a dirt road through the woods. Lila pulls off the road, parks in a place where the car will be camouflaged.

LILA
Stay.

CONTINUED:

Puff stays in the car. Lila gets out, pulls the Lucite mouse case from the back seat.

EXT. LILA'S CAR - EVENING

Lila puts the case on the ground and unlatches it. The mice look confused at first. Then the male mouse pushes the door open and holds it for the female mouse, who exits. The male mouse follows her, and closes the door behind him. He turns to Lila, nods, then extends his arm for the female mouse to hold on to. She does, and they walk off together on their hind legs into the woods. Lila sighs, and turns to Puff.

LILA
Out.

Puff gets out casually, then makes a mad dash for the road. Lila calmly presses the button on her black box. Puff spasms and falls to the ground.

LILA (CONT'D)
Bad.

Puff stays on the ground, breathing hard.

LILA (CONT'D)
Get up.

Puff does.

LILA (CONT'D)
Take off your clothes.

Puff does. So does Lila. But whereas Puff is now white and soft-looking, Lila is tan and taut and muscular. This is a reversal of the way both of them were when they first met. Puff seems taken with her body.

LILA (CONT'D)
We're going back to nature, you and I. I'm going to retrain you. I'm going to make you free again if I have to kill you doing it.

PUFF
But I like being human now.

Lila shocks Puff. He falls to the ground.

LILA
You what?

(CONTINUED)

CONTINUED:

PUFF
I want to be the way I was before.

LILA
(sweet)
Good. I'll show you how.

DISSOLVE TO:

EXT. FOREST - NIGHT

Puff and Lila have built makeshift shelter out of leaves and twigs. They are sitting around a campfire, naked and dirty, roasting a couple of skinned squirrels on sticks. The black box rests in Lila's lap. Puff looks at the roasting squirrel, is repulsed.

PUFF
Nice night.

LILA
Language was invented so people could lie to each other and themselves.

Puff begins to disagree. Lila's hand hovers over the button. He stops himself.

PUFF
(confused)
I agree?

Lila shocks Puff.

LILA
Any answer is the wrong answer.

DISSOLVE TO:

INT. MAKESHIFT SHELTER - NIGHT

Puff and Lila lie separately under blankets of moss. The breathing is heavy. Both seem to be sleeping. Puff opens his eyes and tries to silently extricate himself from the moss. Lila presses the button and Puff falls in a quivering mass. We see this is not easy for her to do to him.

LILA
(whisper)
You'll thank me eventually, Puff.
Y'know, without talking. With, like, a grunt or a snort or something.

(CONTINUED)

CONTINUED:

PUFF
An enchanting picture you paint of our future together.

Lila shocks Puff once again. He spasms.

INT. CONGRESS - DAY

Puff testifies.

PUFF
And so commenced my reeducation, gentlemen. Lila taught me so much. She was a stern but fair teacher. And over time, I began to remember the joy of living in a pure state of being. But something else happened as well, something perhaps distinctly human ... I began to fall in love with Lila.

DISSOLVE TO:

EXT. FOREST - DAY

Lila and Puff are naked and collecting mushrooms and berries. Time has passed. They're both dirty. Puff still wears his collar. Lila bends over to pick a mushroom. Puff looks at her from behind.

PUFF
Boy, you look so good from this ang...

Lila turns, puts her finger to her lips in a gentle "no talking" reminder, then shocks the hell out of Puff. He spasms and falls on top of her, knocking her to the ground. He regains his composure, finds himself on top of Lila. They look at each other for a moment. Then they kiss. It's a violent kiss. They grope each other. This is primal sex now. In the dirt. Sweaty. Loud grunting. Lila even presses the shock button at the right moment. Puff seems to like it in this context.

INT. GABRIELLE'S APT - NIGHT

Nathan and Gabrielle are finishing up polite sex. She pulls herself off. He lies there, faraway. Gabrielle looks over at him.

GABRIELLE
A penny for your thoughts, Mon Cheri.

CONTINUED:

NATHAN
No thoughts.

CUT TO:

INT. NATHAN'S PARENTS' HOUSE - DAY

Gabrielle, Nathan, Nathan's parents, and Wayne eat dinner in silence. Nathan seems far away. Gabrielle watches him, then looks over at Wayne and catches him eyeing her. She winks at the boy. He blushes.

WAYNE
I like the name Gabrielle.

NATHAN
Mother, will you please tell Wayne to stop hitting on my girlfriend.

MOTHER
He's a six year old boy, Nathan. What is wrong with you?

WAYNE
(proudly)
Almost six and a half.

NATHAN
Nothing is wrong with me.

FATHER
I think something is wrong with Nathan.

GABRIELLE
I too, think something is wrong with you, Nathan. You have changed. You are moody. You lash out. I feel when you make love to me, you really make love to someone else.
(to the others)
He hardly looks at me during our lovemaking sessions.
(beat)
Excuse me, this is perhaps not proper to discuss at the table of dinner.

WAYNE
I would never stop looking at you if you were my girl.

Gabrielle smiles at Wayne.

(CONTINUED)

CONTINUED:

NATHAN
He's hitting on her! That's not hitting on her?!

FATHER
Calm down. No one's hitting on anyone.

GABRIELLE
He's just a boy, Nathan. It's you I am worried about. Maybe you could learn something from your brother about how to treat a woman. Do you no longer love me? Or what? Tell me now.

Nathan doesn't say anything. Gabrielle, in tears, runs off. Wayne runs after her.

INT. NATHAN'S BEDROOM - NIGHT

Nathan and Gabrielle are in bed. Both stare up at the ceiling. We move into Nathan's eyes.

DISSOLVE TO:

EXT. ROUSSEAU JUNGLE - NIGHT

There is a quick flash of Nathan kissing and caressing a beautiful, animal-like Lila in a stylized jungle setting.

CUT TO:

INT. NATHAN'S BEDROOM - NIGHT

Nathan and Gabrielle lie in bed staring at the ceiling. Nathan turns to Gabrielle. Nathan kisses her on the cheek.

NATHAN
I want Puff back. I need to find him and bring him back.

GABRIELLE
Oh, Nathan, is that what is bothering you?

NATHAN
Yes. That's what it is.

GABRIELLE
I'm so relieved. I want him back, too! Your brother tonight made me remember how much I miss our own little boy.

CONTINUED:

NATHAN
Did you and Wayne make love?

GABRIELLE
What? What are you talking about?

NATHAN
I'm sorry. It's that Lila. She's driving me crazy. I worked so hard. We worked so hard. Puff would've made us famous. And now he's gone. Because of her.

GABRIELLE
That bitch. She is a hairy bitch!

NATHAN
I'll find her. I need desperately to find her.

Gabrielle looks over at him.

NATHAN (CONT'D)
And bring Puff back.

GABRIELLE
(relieved)
Yes! Yes! Oh, yes! But where do we look for little lost Puff?

NATHAN
I think she is somewhere trying to turn him back into an ape.

GABRIELLE
That is horrible. Apes are dirty. No?

NATHAN
You better believe they're dirty! Dirty and primal and... dirty and...

Nathan, seemingly in the grips of a sudden horrific migraine, scrunches his face and holds his ears. He relaxes a bit, and gets out of bed. He walks across the room, pulls on some pants, and picks up a container called "Stop Buggin' Me, Sunny."

GABRIELLE
I'll pack my sac de couchage. We will be a family once more.

CONTINUED: (2)

NATHAN
(beat)
I'd better go alone. This could be dangerous. I don't want you to get hurt. You are too important to me.

GABRIELLE
I love you again so much now.

INT. NATHAN'S CAR/WOODED ROAD - MORNING

Nathan is driving along a wooded dirt road. He's in his immaculate safari suit. He looks tired. He stops the car, pulls out a gun, and gets out.

EXT. FOREST - MORNING

Nathan gets out of the car and runs into the woods. We follow.

NATHAN
(yelling)
Aha! Just as I suspected!

He looks around there is no one there. He sighs and walks back to his car, pulls out a map and marks an area with a red X.

INT. NATHAN'S APT - NIGHT

Gabrielle, in a T-shirt and shorts, does sit-ups and listens to a tape of Maurice Chevalier singing.

CHEVALIER
Wonderful! Oh, it's wonderful To be in love with you. Beautiful! You're so beautiful, you haunt me all day through

Gabrielle clicks off the tape player and tries the accent.

GABRIELLE
You're so beautiful, You haunt me all day through...
(trying again)
... haunt me all day through... all day through.

She switches on the tape player again.

CHEVALIER
Every little breeze seems to whisper 'Louise. The birds in the trees -- seem to twitter 'Louise'

(CONTINUED)

CONTINUED:

She switches off the tape.

GABRIELLE
The birds in the trees. Birds in the trees seem to twitter 'Louise' Twitter.

The phone rings. Gabrielle heads to the phone.

GABRIELLE (CONT'D)
-- Twitter. Twitter. Twitter. --

Gabrielle picks up the phone.

GABRIELLE (CONT'D)
Yes, what?

INT. NATHAN'S MOTEL ROOM - NIGHT

Nathan is in his underwear. He is ironing his safari suit as he talks on the phone.

NATHAN
Hey.

We see an unfolded map on the bed. There are red X's in almost all the state parks along the east coast.

GABRIELLE (O.S.)
Oh, my wonderful, beautiful Nathan. Did you find our little boy?

NATHAN
No. Not yet. I don't know if I ever will.

GABRIELLE (O.S.)
Oh, my Nathan. I am haunted all day through thinking of you searching alone out there.

NATHAN
It's been hard.

GABRIELLE
Well, at least you have the birds in the trees to twitter at you.

NATHAN
What?

(CONTINUED)

CONTINUED:

GABRIELLE
Nothing. Never mind. I'm just so happy to hear from you. So would you like we should again maybe do a phone sex to help relax you?

NATHAN
Okay.

GABRIELLE (O.S.)
Jungle girl?

NATHAN
Yes, please.

EXT. FOREST - NIGHT

Lila and Puff are having sex again next to a campfire. Now Lila is wearing the collar, and Puff is giving her well timed shocks. They giggle and kiss after they finish. Puff sits up. He holds his stomach and grunts hungrily. Lila grunts back. She stands and retrieves a sack of berries. Puff and Lila greedily, gluttonously stuff their faces. Lila takes some berries and smashes them against Puff's face. She laughs heartily. He looks annoyed for a second, but then grabs a handful and squishes them against Lila's face. Pretty soon they are having a berry war and are covered in purple stains. They hug each other, out of breath and laughing.

INT. INTERROGATION ROOM - NIGHT

Lila smiles.

LILA
It was paradise.
(beat, sadly)
At least for a tiny little while.

EXT. FOREST - DAY

Lila and Puff lie naked in a tree, lazily soaking up the mid-day sun. There is a rustling in the bushes. They both look up, alert but calm. Nathan, immaculate in his safari suit, appears in the clearing. He holds a gun.

NATHAN
Finally. I've covered almost the entire eastern seaboard.

LILA
Ugnh.

(CONTINUED)

CONTINUED:

PUFF
Ugnh.

NATHAN
Oh please, is that as articulate as you can be after all the time I spent teaching you? We've discussed Wittgenstein, for Christ's sake. Not that you ever had anything very challenging to say on the subject.

PUFF
Unn.

NATHAN
Down from the tree.

Lila and Puff climb down from the tree. Nathan watches Lila's muscular, dirty body. He's entranced.

NATHAN (CONT'D)
You both disgust me.

LILA
Oook. Oook.

NATHAN
Shut up!
(to Puff)
I gave you ... life. I took you from this primordial ooze and brought you into the world of culture and manners. And this is how you repay me? I should just leave you here. But I won't. You serve my purpose. And if you had any smarts, you'd realize I serve your purpose as well. Life is so much more delightful lived in a silk suit.

LILA
Ooka.

NATHAN
Don't worry, Lila. I'm only here for Puff. I'm with Gabrielle now. She's a wonderful girl. Not some sweaty, violent, lusty animal, who...

Nathan gets lost in his description of Lila. He looks at her hungrily. Puff looks at Nathan looking at Lila.

NATHAN (CONT'D)
Can I just... touch you, Lila. Just smell you, how you smell now, all dirty and powerful?

Nathan reaches for Lila. She backs away, but is secretly pleased.

NATHAN (CONTÍD)
Please, teach me to be an ape, too. I want to be free, just like anyone else. I do. I'll study really hard. See, I've been practicing. I'm no good yet, but watch. I'm trying.

Nathan tries to act like an ape. It's a repressed version of the excited imitation the young Nathan did at the zoo. Lila watches sadly. Nathan lumbers over to her, tries to smell her, touch her. This is more than Puff can bear. He lunges at Nathan.

PUFF
Nonkaaaa!

The two wrestle on the ground. Puff pries the gun from Nathan's hand, and jumps up. Nathan stands also, backing away. Puff has the gun trained on Nathan. Lila runs to Puff, stands behind him.

NATHAN
Puff, put the gun down.

PUFF
Ounpoo. Ungh.

NATHAN
Let's be reasonable human beings here.

PUFF
(jumping up and down like a chimp)
Unka unka unka unka unka.

NATHAN
Look, you and Lila stay and have your natural life. I'll go. You'll never see me again. I'm no ape. I'm just a guy. Just a plain guy.

PUFF
(to Lila, guiltily)
I have to talk. Is that okay?

CONTINUED: (3)

Lila nods.

PUFF (CONT'D)
Hello, Nathan. Nice to see you. Allow me to explain my position: Before you found me I was a simple, complete being, in harmony with my world. After you, I became duplicitous, anal, totally out of touch with my surroundings. In a word, Nathan, I became you. Lila has reintroduced me to myself.
(to Lila)
Hello, Lila. I love and honor you.

NATHAN
Please don't hurt me --

PUFF
Please don't interrupt me. How very rude of you. Words. Words words words! Words are evil!
(to Lila)
Are not they evil? These words we use?

Lila nods, but nervously. Puff paces

PUFF (CONT'D)
Does anyone know the definition of "simultanagnosia" I was intending to look it up before Lila saved me.

NATHAN
(trying to appease)
It's the inability to perceive elements as components of a whole. Puff thinks about this.

PUFF
Thank you. My pleasure. Don't mention it. Good to see you again. Stop! Okay, now I'm confused. Nothing is right. Please, I need to make sense! Words are wrong! I need need need to make --

NATHAN
Puff, you're agitated --

PUFF
I talk, not you! I! I! I kill you!

NATHAN
No.

PUFF
Yes! And also... I should say... before when I killed, it was for food! Or self-defense! Or...! Now I kill for revenge. Revenge is an abstract concept, Nathan!
(screaming)
I learned abstract thinking from you!

LILA
Puff, don't.

Puff shoots. A hawk screams off-camera. The bullet hits Nathan in the head. He falls. After a moment two mice run past the body.

INT. INTERROGATION ROOM - NIGHT

Lila sobs.

LILA
Then I shot Nathan.

INT. CONGRESS - DAY

Puff dabs his eye.

PUFF
Then Lila shot Nathan.

INT. WHITE SPACE - DAY

Nathan talks.

NATHAN
Then Puff shot me. Then I died. That's all I know. That's the end of my story. Do I go to heaven now?
(beat)
Or is it ... hell?
(beat)
Or ... what?
(beat)
I just stay here? I just stay here and tell it again? And after that? Again? And after ...
(sighs)
Yes. Yes, of course.
(sighs, clears his throat)

CONTINUED:

WE MOVE INTO AN EXTREME CLOSE-UP.

NATHAN (CONT'D)
(beginning again)
I don't even know what sorry means anymore. It's odd. When I was alive I knew -- maybe it's all I knew ...

EXT. FOREST - DAY

Lila runs to Nathan. She kneels beside him.

LILA
He's dead.

PUFF
(calmly)
We bury the body. We disappear into the woods. Nobody knows. There's an off-screen "thonk." A hawk staggers, dazed and unnoticed past Puff and Lila.

LILA
No. It's the end of the road.

PUFF
Forget him, Lila. We'll disappear. We'll never talk about it again. We'll never talk again period. I love you.

LILA
I love you. But they'll find us, Puff. Nathan found us. And we'll go to jail.

PUFF
Jail. Lock-up. The can. Alcatraz. I've seen it depicted in movies and television. Akin to my Lucite case, yes?

There is a long pause as Lila takes this in. Then:

LILA
Oh, God. I put you in that case, Puff. I'm as guilty as Nathan. More!
(decisively)
I'm turning myself in for the murder.

PUFF
I won't let you do that. I shot the bastard. And I'm glad.

CONTINUED:

LILA
I have to! I want to. Please, Puff.
Stay here and live your life.

PUFF
(beat)
Then I'll live it for both of us, Lila.
I'll be the most free, truest animal in
the whole forest. For both of us.

LILA
(tearing up)
That's what I'm counting on.
(new thought)
But first... go back, just long enough to
testify before congress about the
waywardness of humankind.

PUFF
Okay, if you think it will help.

INT. PRISON COMMON ROOM - DAY

Lila, now in prison coveralls, sits in a dayroom with other
women convicts. She is watching a TV mounted on the wall.
Puff is testifying.

PUFF
And so, gentlemen, that is my story. I
agreed to testify before this committee
because I hoped to convey to the American
public that there is indeed a paradise
lost. Human beings have become so
enamored of their intellectual prowess
that they've forgotten to look to the
Earth as a teacher. This is hubris, my
friends. And my story of destruction and
betrayal is proof of that. I will keep
my promise to Lila. I will shed this
suit and return to the wilderness. I
will live out my days naked and free.

CONGRESSMAN
Thank you, sir, and God bless you. Your
story has deeply touched us all. We will
pass some legislation addressing this
problem.

PUFF
Thank you. That is all I ask.
(to camera)
Good-bye, Lila.
(MORE)

(CONTINUED)

CONTINUED:

PUFF (CONT'D)
I take you with me in my untamed heart.
Puff stands and exits the auditorium.

Flashbulbs flash.

INT. PRISON COMMON ROOM - DAY

Lila watches Puff on tv exit the auditorium. She wipes a tear from her eye and seems genuinely happy. She looks out a small barred window and sees a bluebird light there, then fly away.

EXT. WASHINGTON STREET - DAY

Puff walks along, a man on a mission. As he walks he sheds articles of clothing. He is followed by reporters and cameramen and celebrity hounds. Soon he is naked.

EXT. WASHINGTON PORCHES - DAY

Puff walks along, naked. People cheer from porches.

EXT. RURAL ROAD - DUSK

Puff walks along. He is still followed by reporters. Cows watch the parade.

EXT. FOREST - EVENING

Puff walks along a dirt road. He is about to disappear into the forest. An older woman rushes out from the crowd.

OLDER WOMAN
Wait!

PUFF
(turning)
Yes?

OLDER WOMAN
I saw you on C-Span. I've been looking for you for thirty years. Then there you were, such a beautiful, beautiful grown man.

The older woman starts to cry.

PUFF
Mother?

OLDER WOMAN
Yes ... Derek.

Puff holds out his hand for her to shake. Flashbulbs flash.

(CONTINUED)

PUFF
(formally)
It's a pleasure to meet you, mother. But I'm an ape like dad was
(checks watch)
And I have to go back into the woods now ... forever

OLDER WOMAN
(resigned)
Yes, I suppose so. I suppose I knew that was going to be what you would say. It's good to see you again though.

PUFF
Yes.

OLDER WOMAN
I'm in the book, if you ever want to drop me a line or something.

PUFF
I'm an ape, mom. I'm an ape. And apes don't drop lines.

His mother weeps. Puff gently rests his hand on her shoulder for a moment, then he turns and waves to the reporters. The crowd bursts into applause. Flashbulbs flash. Puff jogs into the woods. There is a collective sigh, and then everyone turns and heads back in the direction from which they came. We hold on the woods for a moment. A car pulls up. Puff hurries out of the woods and jumps in the passenger side of the car.

INT. GABRIELLE'S CAR - EVENING

Puff leans over and kisses Gabrielle, who is driving the car.

GABRIELLE
Hello, my little boy.

PUFF
Hey, ma. Did you bring any clothes? I'm freezing my ass off.

GABRIELLE
Oui. Nathan's silk suit.

PUFF
Sweet.
(putting on suit)
God, I've wanted you forever.

CONTINUED:

Gabrielle giggles. Puff kisses her.

GABRIELLE
Say my name.

PUFF
Gabrielle.

GABRIELLE
(eyes glistening)
You remind me so much of Nathan.

PUFF
Like father, like son.

GABRIELLE
(stroking his face)
You remind me so much of Nathan plus so much of my little mongrel doggie.

PUFF
Woof.

This turns Gabrielle on. She kisses him passionately. When the kiss runs its course, Puff speaks.

PUFF (CONT'D)
Arf.

Gabrielle kisses him again, even more passionately this time.

PUFF (CONT'D)
As much as I loved Nathan, I'm not sorry she killed him, if it means I can have you. Is that a terrible thing to say?

GABRIELLE
(putting a finger to his lips)
It is never terrible to be in love.

They smile flirtatiously at each other. Puff leans over and kisses Gabrielle's neck.

PUFF
Let's go eat, I'm starved.

GABRIELLE
French?

PUFF
Oui.

CONTINUED: (2)

They drive off. Puff's smile fades as he watches the passing forest. He sees the leaf and twig shelter that he and Lila had built. He stares at it until it's gone from view.

EXT. EDGE OF FOREST - EVENING

The car speeds past, raising a cloud of dust on the road. When the dust clears, we see the two white mice standing there on the side of the road, shivering and emaciated. The male holds out his thumb and the female holds a tiny little sign which reads: New York. There is a look of hopelessness in their beady black eyes.

FADE OUT

Lila sings over the end credits.

LILA
As I lie/here now/all alone/eyes close/Gone now
I feel the breeze/because you are with me/I see the trees/the leaves rippling in the sun/long as you're here with me We walk along/through fields of rue and heather/We'll sing our song/of love and eternity/I will not look away You are me/so I'm free/these prison halls and walls disappear/I am you/I'm not blue/the forest primeval is right here/Run far away/No, you don't have to stay/because wherever you go is here
I will be with you forever/because you let me in your heart/and I am/here now

THE END

Photograph by Elissa Groh

Writer Dave Franklin met with Charlie Kaufman on February 10, 2002, for the following interview.

Q: Why write *Human Nature* after *Being John Malkovich*? Is it a response to the first film?

My goal, after *Malkovich*, was to get right back to work. I didn't want to wait around thinking about it, worrying about what was expected of me. I mean, *Being John Malkovich*, was a big motherfucker to write. And it was received critically in a big motherfucking way, so I just felt I had to get in there and do something else, rather than be paralyzed by the notoriety. So I thought, shit, I'll write a small movie and it'll be about love, because I was falling in love at the time [with actress Mercedes Ruehl], and I wanted to celebrate that and at the same time look at relationships realistically. I wanted to do all this without the shackles of portals or head invasions or any of the surreal trappings of *Malkovich*. Because that was a cop-out, maybe.

Q: Head invasions were a cop-out?

Well, maybe not really. But it does change the landscape when you don't allow yourself those indulgences. I don't want to come out of the gate every time being the guy who does movies about portals or John Malkoviches or anything else, for that matter. I want each movie experience to be fresh and exciting. For me, and then for the audience.

Q: Was there a first idea or image that got you started with *Human Nature*?

Absolutely. It's the moment when Lila buys that wetsuit. It was ultimately cut from the script, but that was the impetus for the whole project. I remember thinking about a woman, at the time she was called Aggie, going into a dressing room to try on a wetsuit. It was such a metaphorically ripe image for me. It was overripe, really, practically dripping with associations. And I saw the saleslady speaking to her through the dark burgundy curtain, saying, "Does it fit?," which, I mean, I love that line: "Does it fit?" Now it's not in the movie. I guess I'm going to use it in something else. The whole scene. Maybe I'll resurrect the name Aggie, too, since I didn't use it this time around either. Who knows?

Q: What about the title of the movie? How did that come about?
It was the second thing I thought of, after Aggie in the wetsuit. I don't know. *Human Nature.* I guess I liked it because it was so motherfucking huge a concept. I mean, what is human nature? It's every goddamn thing in the world. And I liked that. That spoke to me.

Q: You've been referred to as "a weirdo from weirdtown." What does that mean?
[Laughs.] People have to label, y'know? I don't know what the fuck it means. I do my work. I live a quiet life [with Ruehl and kids Topper and Lena], and I write. That's it. If my imagination is particularly rich, that's a positive thing. Maybe people just need to shoot down things that threaten them. I should do a movie about that. Personally, I don't think of my work as weird. It seems true to me. This is how I see the world. So fuck 'em if they can't take a joke, right? [Laughs.]

Q: What was it that attracted you to the idea of humans as animals in captivity?
I grew up on Salinger. I just loved him. I really related to his characters. And he had this book called *Franny and Zooey*. I was thinking about that at the time, not so much the book, but the title. The word Zooey really interested me mostly. I related to that name. I'd never known anyone with that name. I'd known a couple of Zoe's. But no Zooey, who it turns out, if I remember correctly, was a guy. So I thought, guys in zoos. People in zoos. Then it occurred to me that we all really live in a zoo, if you want to think of human society as a zoo. And I guess it just snowballed from there, really. I thought maybe I had really come up with something. It was a heady time.

Q: For all its dark undercurrents, *Being John Malkovich* was a kick of a movie, very pleasure-filled. Why go so far into despair and darkness this time?
I was taken there by the subject matter. Y'know, these are very dark and despairing issues. Without going into too much personal detail, I was immersed the last few years in lots of sadness, some of it involving an actual feral person. And there's nothing funny about it. I wasn't going to mock it or diminish it by playing it for laughs. Sorry, but the audience is going to have to accept that. Or not. It's complicated.

Q: *Human Nature* is packed with fascinating characters. Could we go through and talk about them one by one? Let's start with Lila Jute.
I know and have known many women like that. Warm, troubled women, with body image problems. Struggling women who have that quirky cadence: begging for love with every utterance. Y'know? They break my heart and I love them dearly. I want to protect them. And as a cineast, it gave me a chance to flex those movie muscles that give voice to the eternal feminine in its uncorrupted form. This is no small feat in a business and culture that systematically devalues the feminine.

Q: Nathan Bronfman?
Long story short, I had been turned onto a cassette of two guys talking, saying things like, "We need to teach table manners to mice." It turns out they were actually quoting a guy named R. Ronald Agnew, a sort of gonzo behavioral scientist who was actually doing this kind of research. Basically trying to destroy nature by controlling it.

And at the same time I was interested in the work of Scott Marcus, the animal trainer from Nashua, New Hampshire. Marcus was training elk to do fucking amazing things. Nobody could believe it: they were doing this tap dancing shit. But he was torturing them, y'know? And I thought, that's so fucked. Anyway, he has these speech patterns and demeanor just like these guys I went to high school with. So I was just *there* immediately, y'know, just fascinated.

And around this same time I got a chance to go to the set of *Arlington Road*, and I met Tim Robbins. You know, you never consider Tim Robbins for one of your movies the way you never consider becoming president of the United States. It just isn't in the cards. But then Tim called me and I thought, oh, God, I really want to use this opportunity. It was such a fucking amazing opportunity and I went and ran with it, trying to create a role for Tim that would impress the shit out of him.

Q: Is there a way Nathan is related to Craig in *Being John Malkovich*?
Probably so, in the sense of his being an outsider like Craig. And that both guys are trying to be puppeteers, in a way. Nathan with mice and also with Puff. Craig with puppets, which is, I guess, more of a literal way of being a puppeteer, but I see a correlation. In, like, controlling people. Or animals. It's fucking brutal.

Q: What about Puff? You mentioned him just now, so we maybe should go to him next.
I've always loved Spielberg's portrayal of children. Only Salinger had been able to find that complexity. And when I saw Anna Pacquin in *The Piano*, I realized a kid could be so deep and fascinating. It was, like, a revelation, because normally you think of kids as just there, just things that play and cry. I wanted to investigate this new world.

Add to that all the pressure I felt with *Malkovich* coming out and all these people watching me and all my goddamn hours on the shrink's couch being psychoanalyzed, and I'm thinking, God, I'm way too much of a kid myself to have this kind of pressure, to have to be in this position. But at the same time I wanted it so badly.

On top of that, I had recently met Mercedes, and she had told me this story about when she was a younger actress, just starting out, and she had to learn how to walk in some period costume, like a hoop skirt. She had never had any training in that and she had to, like, go through a "culture" boot camp, but after work, she just wanted to hang out in the woods. She was, like, motherfucking split in two directions. Here she was, this kid, this innocent, but she also knew she had to learn these things to be sophisticated, to be a great actress. And that's what I ended up going for with Puff, that sense of a little kid, forced to grow up. He even dresses as Peter Pan in one scene.

And also, because Puff was so naïve and childlike at first, it gave me an opportunity to write really direct, basic, emotionally-clean lines, like "I am Puff," which, y'know, is about as clean a thought as a character can express.

Q: Gabrielle?
Well, in one way, Gabrielle is my homage to Charles Boyer [the late, great French actor] and his character in Anatole Litvak's *All This and Heaven Too*,

but I wanted her to be harder, tougher. And I really wanted to write something for Miranda Otto. I'd loved her work, and I wanted to shackle her. By giving her an accent to work with, it was forcing Miranda to be less eloquent and exact. I knew something beautiful would come from that and I was right. And it's funny, because although I've written fucked-up fake French women before, and I will again, Gabrielle is the only one of my characters I truly hate. I loathe her, so much so that I needed to vanquish her to eternal torture at the end of the movie. I couldn't have her getting away. So even though it looks like she's getting away, you can see in her face that she's ruined and she will spend the rest of her life searching in vain for even a moment's peace. "Die, fucker," I'm saying to her, in my way. Or rather, "Die, but don't die, because I want to torture you forever." There's no forgiveness for the character of Gabrielle.

Q: Louise?
It's a study of the child actress grown up to be an electrologist. It's "How did I get here?" It's fucking sad and also very, very fucking true. It pains me.

Q: Nathan's Mom?
Yeah, Mrs. Bronfman. That one's simple. Mary Kay Place played Floris in *Malkovich*. And we hung out a lot and she's great. She gets cast often in kind of kooky roles, and I wanted her to play something closer to who she really is: a decent, warm, caring mother-type, who maybe cries too much at sappy TV movies. I wanted to bring that sweetness to Mary Kay's part and that's why I wrote the mother as I did. That character always makes me cry. I love her.

Q: Nathan's Dad?
This came out of a time when Bob Forster and I were working together on a movie, and I was getting really screwed by the producers. We were just goofing around with a video camera, kind of just trying to ease the tension and sadness. Bob was pretending to be a 1950s father and it was hysterical—fucking amazing. That guy can act. And I wanted to use it, to do something with that character, but take it further, y'know? To take the stereotype of that father and show the loneliness, the true horror of his existence. What was it really like to live in the fifties? I had to find out. Those kind of questions kept coming up while I was writing. At the same time, I wanted to have Bob Forster in an ascot. I really wanted that. It was as important to me

as anything else in the script. But that's an intuitive thing. I can't defend it, except to say, watch the movie. I think I was right.

Q: The cops?

I truly love the cops. My affection for them is just enormous. And I worry that there may be a lack of connection by audiences, because when you first see them, they're interrogating Lila, who the audience adores. But I had an enormous desire to write those characters as truthfully as possible, because I have known cops. I've known so many cops over the years, and having seen representations of cops in the cinema before, I wanted to take it to a new level, to get some subtlety and truth in there—to get something that might have previously been lost on mass audiences. Of course they fight crime. That's a given and a non-issue. What else? Dig deeper. What makes cops happy? What do they cry out during long, sweaty sleepless nights? How have the cops' hearts been broken? So when the cops have trouble listening, really listening to Lila's story, I want the audience to say, yes, they are incapable of hearing her pain and I know why.

I also wrote the parts for Ken Magee, Sy Richardson, and David Warshofsky. We've been friends forever. I wanted to write something great and star-making for them: I wanted to be their lovers, in a movie-making way. They turned out to be my favorite performances in the film.

Q: Do you have any designs on directing?

[Long pause.] This is the part of interview where you'll be writing "long pause" in brackets. [Laughs.] Then you'll be writing "laughs" because I just don't know how to answer this. I am a writer, first and foremost... But as I think about it, I have to say I am a filmmaker first and foremost. And as a filmmaker, I have to consider taking the vision from its inception to its finish. Maybe this is the way to truly fulfill the promise of my scripts. Which is not to say I don't value the work of the directors I've collaborated with. I do. They are fucking awesome motherfuckers. But I need to bring the rest of myself to the world. And I will.

Q: How did you decide to make Bonnie Raitt's songs a character in the film?

Bonnie is so fucking cool, and I wanted everyone to know that I think so. Specifically though, it's that line from her song "Magic Hour": "What does it mean to be civilized and how can I never, ever find out?" So much stemmed from that for me.

Bonnie's songs are about the nature of love and the love of nature, the nature of nature, and the love of being in love. What the fuck else is there? [Laughs.] Her lyrics are both tragic and uplifting and beautiful and nasty. And I wanted that in my movie. Bonnie is the person who turned me on to thinking about the big questions: What is life? Where is life? Why can't we love well? It was Bonnie and Mercedes who taught me how fucking hard it is to be in love and how much it's worth it. I love them both, and I want everyone to know. That's why.

Q: This must be related to the scene where all the characters begin singing along with one of Bonnie Raitt's songs.
"Please Hurt Me" is the song and the line is "Please, for the love of God, show me the way." I can absolutely remember the moment when I wrote that scene. I was going through some of my own shit then. Personal stuff that I won't go into here. But I sat down to write it and all this stuff was coming together in the movie, and I just started to cry, as I was writing. Usually when you're writing a scene it's very technical: figuring out dialogue, punchlines, arcs, but I just thought, "All the characters have to sing here." And so, fuck it, I just wrote it that way. As a cineast I can relate to that truth: people sing when they're in trouble. They listen to their favorite song on the radio and they sing and they cry and it's just raw and true. And I needed that in the film at that point. I needed it in my motherfucking life, too.

Q: Of all things, why frogs?
Oh, the frogs falling from the sky! The question of the ages! [Laughs.] Well, I just liked the idea. I read about it. It really happens! So that was the initial reason; it just seemed cool, but then as I thought about it, I realized how it fit into my story. Because it's, like, if it's raining frogs, then there's no sense to anything. Nothing you believed to be true holds. And I wanted to look at that and, more importantly, force the audience to sit with that thought: that there is an irrationality to all of our lives and until something so out of the norm happens, we can't see that. I want people to see it and think about it. And frogs are green, which is the color of nature. So in a way frogs represent the natural world and I'm saying, "Look, the natural world is falling the fuck on top of you. Look up, goddamn it, and take notice."

Q: What made you decide to use sequences of weird historical coincidences as a framing device for the film?
It's a promise. A promise to my audience. I'm saying, look at these stories. They're all weird and bizarre and maybe true or maybe not, but, hey, if you give me four hours, I will give you a story just as weird and wonderful and amazing as these stories, because this stuff does happen in the world. Y'know? The world is bigger than we think.

Q: Is the end of the film cathartic or unresolved? Is there some hope at the end of the day? Or will the sadness just go on and on?
For me it's totally cathartic! It's hopeful and wonderful and I cry whenever I see the movie for that reason. But of course it's sad, too. And I cry about that as well. For Mercedes and me it's important to look at the whole spectrum of feelings that any situation creates. Love is great, but it's also hard as shit. It's a lot of work and sweaty and embarrassing. But the surrender to it is so beautiful. What else is there, really?

The problem with traditional movies is they usually have to have it one way or the other: happy or sad. For those people who need it, we have a happy ending, but for people who want to look deeper, the movie is saying, yes, love is real, but the road to it is complicated and you're going to make terrible messes along the way and you need to go on anyway.

My goal in my work is to show that motherfucking paradox, because I believe that it is in this paradox that you find life. That is what my work, at least at this point, is really about. It's complicated, y'know? Life is fucking complicated. Too many filmmakers don't want to deal with that. They want to dumb down their vision for mass consumption. Listen, I don't think it's an accident that film is an art form that utilizes the lens. Filmmakers are the eyes of a society. We see and we reflect. We need to show what is wrong and painful. But a true lens is all encompassing; it also shows all the motherfucking hope and beauty in the world.

FINE LINE FEATURES AND STUDIOCANAL PRESENT
A GOOD MACHINE PRODUCTION
IN ASSOCIATION WITH BEVERLY DETROIT STUDIOS AND PARTIZAN

TIM ROBBINS PATRICIA ARQUETTE RHYS IFANS MIRANDA OTTO

HUMAN NATURE

ROSIE PEREZ

CASTING BY JEANNE McCARTHY
COSTUME DESIGNER NANCY STEINER
MUSIC SUPERVISOR TRACY McKNIGHT
MUSIC BY GRAEME REVELL
EDITOR RUSSELL ICKE
PRODUCTION DESIGNER K.K. BARRETT
DIRECTOR OF PHOTOGRAPHY TIM MAURICE-JONES
CO-PRODUCER JULIE FONG
PRODUCED BY ANTHONY BREGMAN TED HOPE
SPIKE JONZE CHARLIE KAUFMAN
WRITTEN BY CHARLIE KAUFMAN
DIRECTED BY MICHEL GONDRY

LILA JUTE . . . . Patricia Arquette
PUFF . . . . Rhys Ifans
NATHAN BRONFMAN . . . . Tim Robbins
POLICE DETECTIVES . . . . Ken Magee
Sy Richardson
David Warshofsky
YOUNG LILA . . . . Hilary Duff
DOCTOR . . . . Stanley Desantis
FRANK . . . . Peter Dinklage
PUFF'S FATHER . . . . Toby Huss
CONGRESSMEN . . . . Bobby Harwell
Daryl Anderson
YOUNG PUFF . . . . Bobby Pyle
YOUNG NATHAN . . . . Chase Bebak
NATHAN'S MOTHER . . . . Mary Kay Place
NATHAN'S FATHER . . . . Robert Forster
LOUISE . . . . Rosie Perez
WENDALL THE THERAPIST . . . . Miguel Sandoval
GABRIELLE . . . . Miranda Otto
WAYNE BRONFMAN . . . . Anthony Winsick
BISTRO WAITRESS . . . . Mary Portser
AVERSION THERAPY MODEL . . . Laura Grady Peterson
CHESTER'S WAITRESS . . . . Angela Little
STRIPPER . . . . Deborah Ferrari
LECTURE HOST . . . . Jeremy Kramer
PUFF'S MOTHER . . . . Nancy Lenehan

STUNT COORDINATOR . . . . Eddie Perez
STUNT PLAYERS . . . . Al Goto
Joni Avery
Tim Rigby
Jimmy Romano
Jared Eddo
CHOREOGRAPHER . . . . John Cassese
The Dance Doctor
UNIT PRODUCTION MANAGER . . . . . . Gilly Ruben
FIRST ASSISTANT DIRECTOR . . Haze J.F. Bergeron, III
SECOND ASSISTANT DIRECTOR . . . . . Otto Penzato

CAMERA OPERATOR . . . . Tom Lohmann
FIRST ASSISTANT CAMERA . . . . Mike Lohmann
SECOND ASSISTANT CAMERA . . . . Lilith Simcox
CAMERA LOADER . . . . Tim Sheridan
B CAMERA FIRST ASSISTANT . . . . Cal Roberts
STILL PHOTOGRAPHER . . . . Bruce Birmelin
HD CAMERA TECHNICIAN. . . . . Sean Fairburn
CAMERA PRODUCTION ASSISTANT . . . . Sam Spiegel
CAMERA DEPARTMENT INTERN . . . . . . Julia Means

CONTINUITY SUPERVISOR . . . . Aaron Kisner

PRODUCTION SOUND MIXER . . . . Drew Kunin
BOOM OPERATOR . . . . Larry Commans
UTILITY SOUND TECHNICIAN . . . . . . Fred Johnston

ART DIRECTOR . . . . Peter Andrus
ART DEPARTMENT COORDINATORS . . Aimee Rousey
Patty Mcnulty
ART DEPARTMENT PRODUCTION ASSISTANT . . .
Adrianna Lopez-Cook

SET DESIGNERS . . . . Sloane U'ren
Fanée Aaron
SET DECORATOR . . . . Gene Serdena
LEADMAN . . . . Grant D. Samson
ON-SET DRESSER . . . . Christian Kastner
BUYER . . . . Robert Stover
SET DRESSERS . . . . Bobby Pollard
Jamie Fleming
Robert Anderson
J. Michael Glynn
Paul Manion

PROPERTY MASTER . . . . Jeffrey M. O'brien
ASSISTANT PROPERTY MASTER . . . . . . Keith Wood
ASSISTANT PROPS . . . . Carly Brullo-Niles
Tanya Magidow

CHIEF LIGHTING TECHNICIAN . . . . . Brian T. Louks
ASSISTANT CHIEF LIGHTING TECHNICIAN . . . . .
Steve Galvin
ELECTRICIANS . . . . Jim Vititoe
Matthew Bardocz
Greg Mayer
ADDITIONAL ELECTRICIAN . . . . . . Chris Hathaway
RIGGING GAFFER . . . . Oscar Rodriguez

KEY GRIP . . . . Vincent M. Palomino
BEST BOY GRIP . . . . Shannon Summers
DOLLY GRIPS . . . . Robert Foster
Sid Hajdu
GRIPS . . . . George Canaday
David Palmieri
George Gregory
Joe Tawater
KEY RIGGING GRIP . . . . Pat Webb
BEST BOY RIGGING GRIP . . . . Mike Lavere

COSTUME SUPERVISOR . . . . Marina Marit
SET COSTUMER . . . . Anita Brown
ASSISTANT COSTUME DESIGNER . . . . Jennifer Dozier
COSTUME PRODUCTION ASSISTANT . . . Karen Baird

BODY HAIR EFFECTS CREATED BY . . . Tony Gardner
Alterian Studios
ALTERIAN PROJECT SUPERVISOR . . . Connie Grayson
PROSTHETIC MAKE-UP . . . . Barney Burman

MAKE-UP DEPARTMENT HEAD . . . . Roz Music
KEY MAKE-UP/TIM ROBBINS . . . . Luisa Abel
ADDITIONAL MAKE-UP . . . . Sheri Knight

KEY HAIRSTYLIST . . . . Janis Clark
ASSISTANT HAIRSTYLIST . . . . Susan Maust

LOCATION MANAGER . . . . Deborah J. Page
ASSISTANT LOCATION MANAGER . . Ernest T. Belding
LOCATION ASSISTANT . . . . Donny Martino, Jr.
LOCATION SCOUTS . . . . Serena Baker
Doug Mcclintock
Matt Cassel

PRODUCTION ACCOUNTANT . . Mindy Sheldon-Barry
FIRST ASSISTANT ACCOUNTANT . . . . . Aillene Bubis
SECOND ASSISTANT ACCOUNTANT . . . . Nick Irwin
PAYROLL ACCOUNTANT . . . . Jeff Gladu

PRODUCTION COORDINATOR . . . . . Kait Pickering
ASSISTANT PRODUCTION COORDINATOR . . . . .
Wendy Harrold
OFFICE PRODUCTION ASSISTANTS . . . Mary Allison
John Watkinson
OFFICE INTERNS . . . . Clement Jolin
Michelle Li

CASTING ASSOCIATE . . . . Blythe Cappello
CASTING INTERNS . . . . John Srednicki
Nadia Lubbe
Stacy Jorgensen
Debbie Amler
DIALECT COACH . . . . Judi Dickerson
EXTRAS CASTING DIRECTOR . . . . Sande Alessi
EXTRAS CASTING ASSOCIATE . . . . . . Kristan Berona
ELECTROLYSIS CONSULTANT . . . . . . Sabrina Smith

SET MEDICS . . . . Tony Whitmore
Gary Kurashige
CONSTRUCTION MEDIC . . . . Ahmed Saker

CONSTRUCTION COORDINATOR . . . . Chris Forster
LEAD SET PAINTER . . . . Michael Leblovic
GENERAL FOREMAN . . . . Scott Head

PROPMAKERS

Gregory Paul	Austin Robert Brown
Chris Lee	Chris Mccann
Anders Rundblad	Martin Russell
Andrew Schultz	Daron Smith
Debra Yukelson	

PAINTER FOREMAN . . . . David Steiner

SET PAINTERS

David Carberry	Hector Fernandez
Scott Valdes	Shelly Chamberlain
David Valdes	Charisse St. Amant

LABOR FOREMAN . . . . Robert Davis

LABORERS

Steven Cook
Gary Stel
Kenneth White
Don Tucker

GREENS FOREMAN . . . . Porfirio Silva

GREENS

Jamie Galindo
Robert Neves
Jess Anscott
Jose Orozco
Jamie Castellanos
Rod Gregory
Jon Krueger

SPECIAL EFFECTS COORDINATOR . . Robert Milstein
SPECIAL EFFECTS SUPERVISOR . . . . Phil Bartko
SPECIAL EFFECTS FOREMAN . . . . Boyd La Cosse
SPECIAL EFFECTS TECHNICIAN . . . . . . Harley Riker

CRAFT SERVICE . . . . Nancy James
ADDITIONAL CRAFT SERVICE . . . . . Charles Weaver
ASSISTANT CRAFT SERVICE . . . . Michael Mosley
Hoppy Munz

TRANSPORTATION COORDINATOR . . Griff Ruggles
TRANSPORTATION CAPTAIN . . . . . . Krister Johnson

DRIVERS

Michael "Crash" Anderson
John Simanouich
Buster Videgain
Morgan Mcguinness
David Hernandez
Pablo Gonzalez
Jim Moores
Michael Dawson
Glen Mcraven
Greg Bauer
James Biehahn
Craig Williams
Rick Whitesman
Scott Visser
Ronald Stinton
James Boniface

SECOND SECOND ASSISTANT DIRECTOR . . . . . .
Carolyn Fine
KEY SET PRODUCTION ASSISTANT . . Harry Fitzpatrick
SET PRODUCTION ASSISTANTS . . . . Ron Pogue
Andrew Fox
SET INTERN . . . . Fernanda Cardoso

ASSISTANT TO MICHEL GONDRY . . . . Phil Klemmer
ASSISTANT TO ANTHONY BREGMAN . . . .
Emma Wilcockson
ASSISTANT TO JULIE FONG . . . . Sean Gilleland
ASSISTANT TO TED HOPE . . . . Jennifer Porst
ASSISTANT TO SPIKE JONZE . . . . Howard Shur
CAST PRODUCTION ASSISTANTS . . . . Krista Thomas
Joanna Murphy
Tony Mezzapelle

MR. ROBBINS' STAND-IN . . . . David Maier
MS. ARQUETTE'S STAND-IN . . . . Kelly O'quinn
MR. IFANS' STAND-IN . . . . Brian Galyean
MS. OTTO'S STAND-IN . . . . Joy Highsmith

ANIMALS SUPPLIED BY . . . .
Animal Actors Of Hollywood, Inc.
Benay's Bird And Animal Source
LEAD MOUSE TRAINERS . . . . . . Doree Sitterly Bayliss
Veronica Wise

ANIMAL TRAINERS

Deborah Brighton
Christie Miele
Trish Peebles
Mark Jackson
Lara Osborn
Cheryl Shawver

CATERING . . . . Tony's Food Service
Neda Kerum
Ante Topic
Leo Loera

ANIMATION UNIT

MINIATURE ANIMATION CREATED BY . . Holy Cow
ANIMATION SUPERVISOR . . . . Shaun Sewter
ANIMATOR . . . . Anthony Farquhar-Smith
MINIATURE CONSTRUCTION . . . . Gary Smith
MINIATURE SET DECORATOR . . . . . . Laura Plansker
MINIATURE GAFFER . . . . Shawn Holoubek
ASSISTANT MINIATURE SET DECORATOR . . . . . .
Wendy Hyde

SECOND UNIT

CAMERA OPERATOR . . . . Tom Lohmann
Eric D. Andersen
FIRST ASSISTANT CAMERA . . . . Mike Lohmann
Dave Taylor
SECOND ASSISTANT CAMERA . . . . . Mark Sasabuchi
LOADER . . . . Brian Breithaupt
GAFFER . . . . Brian T. Louks
Scott Moody
BEST BOY ELECTRIC . . . . Billy Gunn
KEY GRIP . . . . Matthew Blum
BEST BOY GRIP . . . . Calvin Starnes
DOLLY GRIP . . . . Ricky Ellis
GRIP . . . . David Palmieri
CAMERA PRODUCTION ASSISTANT . . Michael Brady
ART DEPARTMENT . . . . Gary Smith
PRODUCTION SUPERVISOR . . . . Zoe Odlum
KEY SET PRODUCTION ASSISTANTS . . Aaron Kampfer
Ron Pogue
PRODUCTION ASSISTANT . . . . Eric Grush

POST PRODUCTION

POST PRODUCTION SUPERVISOR . . Emma Wilcockson

FIRST ASSISTANT EDITOR . . . . Jeff Mcevoy

VISUAL FX AND MOUSE ANIMATION . . . . Buf
CG SUPERVISOR . . . . Geoffrey Niquet

COMPUTER GRAPHISTS

Xavier Allard
Ferdinand Boutard
Jean-François D'izarny
Olivier Dumont
Anthony Liant
Pierre Avon
Amidhou Liazidi
Olivier Cauwet
Yann Blondel

BUF PRODUCTION . . . . Valerie Delahaye
Fabienne Reilly
Anne Gros Lafaige
SOFTWARE/RENDERING . . . . Mental Image
LA OFFICE MANAGER . . . . Nadine Le Gouguec

LEAD RE-RECORDING MIXER . . . . John Ross
RE-RECORDING MIXERS . . . . Dave Bach
Joe Barnett
Warren Kleiman
John Reese
Yuri Reese
Bill Smith

SUPERVISING SOUND EDITORS . . . . . Walter Spencer
Francois Blaignan

SUPERVISING SOUND DESIGNER . . . Claude Letessier
DIALOG & ADR EDITOR . . . . Walter Spencer
SOUND EDITORS . . . . John Reese
Gregoire Couzinier
ASSISTANT DIALOG EDITOR . . . . Greg Tenbosch
FOLEY ARTIST . . . . John Post

SOUND EDITING FACILITY . . . . Nomad
SOUND DESIGN FACILITY . . . . Primal Scream
SOUND MIX FACILITIES . . . . . Digital Sound & Picture
Warrenwood Sound Studios

SCORE ARRANGED AND PRODUCED BY . . . .
Graeme Revell

RECORDED AT . . . . Bolero Studios & Studio X
MUSIC PROGRAMMER . . . . David Russo
ORCHESTRATER . . . . Tim Simonec
COPYIST . . . . Gregg Nestor
SCORING MIXER . . . . Steve Smith
MIX ENGINEER . . . . Mark Curry
MUSIC EDITOR . . . . Ashley Revell
TEMP MUSIC EDITORS . . . . Zig Gron
Roy Prendergast
ADDITIONAL SOURCE MUSIC EDITOR . Brian Bulman
SCORE PREMIX SERVICES . . . . Larry Mah

NEGATIVE CONFORM . . . . Executive Cutting Services
FILM LABORATORY . . . . Fotokem Industries, Inc.
DUBBING FACILITIES . . . . Sound Services, Inc.
DOLBY SOUND CONSULTANT . . . . . . James Wright

ASSISTANT EDITOR (PRODUCTION) . Debra Goldfield

FILM CONFORM EDITORS . . . . Kristin Eaton
Bret Marnell
Hope Moskowitz
Maggie Ostroff
Stefanie Wiseman

POST PRODUCTION COORDINATOR . . . Ron Pogue
POST PRODUCTION ASSISTANTS . . Mark Cabalquinto
Michelle Li
ADDITIONAL GRAPHICS . . . . . Herve De Crecy (H5)
Ludovic Houplain
Brian Smallwork

ADDITIONAL VFX SHOT . . . . Method
METHOD CG DESIGNER . . . . Olivier "Twist" Gondry
METHOD VISUAL EFFECTS PRODUCER Paul Perez Hahn
METHOD INFERNO ARTIST . . . . Scott Mcneil
METHOD DIRECTOR OF TECHNOLOGY . . . .
Andreas Wacker
METHOD EXECUTIVE PRODUCER . Neysa Horsburgh

FINANCING PROVIDED BY . . . . Natexis Banque
Bennett Pozil

PRODUCTION BANKING . . . .
Republic Bank California, N.A.

COMPLETION BOND . . . . Film Finances
Maureen Duffy
Paula Schmit
Greg Trattner
Kurt Wolner

LEGAL COUNSEL . . . . Susan Bodine
Alison Cohen
Epstein, Levinsohn, Bodine,
Hurwitz & Weinstein, Llp.

INSURANCE . . . . Ross Miller
D.R. Reiff & Associates

UNIT PUBLICITY . . . . MPRM Public Relations

LABORATORY . . . . Fotokem Laboratories
FOTOKEM COORDINATOR . . . . Carol Hopkins
COLOR TIMER . . . . Mato

TELECINE DAILIES SERVICES . . . . Level 3 Post
LIGHTING & GRIP EQUIPMENT PROVIDED BY . . .
Paskal Lighting
ARRIFLEX CAMERAS BY . . . . Otto Nemenz
SPECIAL CAMERA EQUIPMENT BY . . . .
Geofilm Group, Inc.
24P DIGITAL TECHNOLOGY . . . . . . Sony Electronics
VIDEO PLAYBACK . . . . Playback Technologies, Inc.
REAR PROJECTION . . . . . Gearhouse Los Angeles, Inc.
FILM STOCK . . . . Fuji Film

PRODUCTION FACILITIES AND STAGES . . . . Playa Vista Stages
POST-PRODUCTION FACILITIES . . . . Buf
AVID SYSTEMS PROVIDED BY . . . . D.E.S.
OPTICALS . . . . Title House Digital
Stewart Motion Picture Services
DIGITAL OPTICALS BY . . . . Digital Film Labs
DIGITAL OPTICALS ARTIST . . . . Dan Walker Arquette
TITLE DESIGN . . . . Buf
DIGITAL FILM RECORDING . . . . Duboi, PARIS
DIGITAL FILM SCANNING . . . . E.Films
Cinesite

MUSIC

"Hair Everywhere"
LYRICS BY CHARLIE KAUFMAN
MUSIC AND ORCHESTRATIONS BY JEAN-MICHEL BERNARD
PERFORMED BY PATRICIA ARQUETTE

"Snow"
WRITTEN BY ELAYNE ROBERTS
AND FLORENCE ROBERTS
PERFORMED BY MARTY AND ELAYNE ROBERTS
PUBLISHED BY ELAYNE ROBERTS/FLORENCE
ROBERTS PUBLISHING DESIGNEE
COURTESY OF ENTERPRISE RECORDS

"You"
WRITTEN BY ELAYNE ROBERTS
AND FLORENCE ROBERTS
PERFORMED BY MARTY AND ELAYNE ROBERTS
PUBLISHED BY ELAYNE ROBERTS/FLORENCE
ROBERTS PUBLISHING DESIGNEE
COURTESY OF ENTERPRISE RECORDS

"Me And Bobby Mcgee"
WRITTEN BY KRIS KRISTOFFERSON
AND FRED FOSTER
PERFORMED BY TIM ROBBINS
USED BY PERMISSION OF COMBINE MUSIC CORP.

"Fais Do Do"
PERFORMED BY MIRANDA OTTO
TRADITIONAL

"Waltzes No's 3, 4, 6 & 12"
WRITTEN BY FRANZ SCHUBERT
ARRANGED BY GEORGE WILSON
PUBLISHED BY CARBERT SPECIAL ACCOUNTS
COURTESY OF ASSOCIATED PRODUCTION MUSIC

"I've Gotta Crow"
WRITTEN BY CAROLYN LEIGH
AND MARK CHARLAP
PERFORMED BY RHYS IFANS
PUBLISHED BY EDWIN H. MORRIS & COMPANY,
A DIVISION OF MPL COMMUNICATIONS, INC./
USED BY PERMISSION OF CARWIN MUSIC INC.

"Supper Club Piano"
WRITTEN BY ROBERT J. WALSH,
WILLIAM ROGOWSKI
PUBLISHED BY FIRST DIGITAL MUSIC
COURTESY OF FIRSTCOM MUSIC, INC.
A ZOMBA COMPANY

"Orpheus & Eurydike"
WRITTEN BY CHRISTOPHER W. GLUCK
PUBLISHED BY SONIA/APM
COURTESY OF ASSOCIATED PRODUCTION MUSIC

"Memories Of You"
WRITTEN BY ROBERT J. WALSH
PUBLISHED BY FIRST DIGITAL MUSIC
COURTESY OF FIRSTCOM MUSIC, INC.
A ZOMBA COMPANY

"Allegretto In B Flat Major"
WRITTEN BY LUDWIG VAN BEETHOVEN
PRODUCED AND PERFORMED BY
JEAN-MICHEL BERNARD (PIANO)
WITH F. LAROQUE (VIOLIN) AND JP AUDIN (CELLO)
SOUND ENGINEER: RODOLPHE GERVAIS
RECORDED AT POPION STUDIO, FRANCE

"El Internado"
WRITTEN BY FRANCISCO CANARO
PERFORMED BY THE SEXTETO MAYOR ORCHESTRA
PUBISHED BY BMG SONGS, INC. O/B/O BMG RELAY
EDICTONES MUSICALES
COURTESY OF ANGEL RECORDS
UNDER LICENSE FROM EMI-CAPITOL
SPECIAL MARKETS

"Au Dehors Frémit La Pluie"
LYRICS BY FLORENCE FONTAINE
MUSIC AND ORCHESTRATIONS
BY JEAN-MICHEL BERNARD
PERFORMED BY NATHALIE LHERMITTE
JEAN-MICHEL BERNARD (PIANO),
MICHEL GAUCHER (SAX)
SOUND ENGINEER: RODOLPHE GERVAIS
RECORDED AT POPION STUDIO, FRANCE

"Push My Little Car"
WRITTEN AND PERFORMED BY MICHEL GONDRY
AND LISA CROOK

"La Petite Etoile De Septembre"
WRITTEN BY MARIE-NOELLE GONDRY
ARRANGED BY GRAEME REVELL
PUBLISHED BY MARIE-NOELLE GONDRY'S
PUBLISHING DESIGNEE

"Here With You"
LYRICS BY CHARLIE KAUFMAN
MUSIC AND ORCHESTRATIONS BY
JEAN-MICHEL BERNARD
PERFORMED BY PATRICIA ARQUETTE

ART DEPARTMENT
The Minneapolis Institute Of Arts
THE PUSHOVER FILM CLIP & PROPS COURTESY OF
Wicked Pictures
Doc Johnson Enterprises
Las Vegas Novelties
Bordighera, 1884, CLAUDE MONET © 2000
THE ART INSTITUTE OF CHICAGO.
ALL RIGHTS RESERVED

SPECIAL THANKS

Buf
Georges Bermann
Scott Carlton
Roman Coppola
Nicole Dionne
Gina Fortunato
Jordan Freid
David Hayes
Jean Kleiman
Amy Lillard
Chris Nadel
Larry Thorpe
Joey Waronker

Danny Benair
Kimiko Bernard
Tim Clawson
Carl Cresser
Jean-Pierre Dionnet
Melissa Fox
Evan Green
Laura Kim
Vincent Landay
Tom Muldoon
John Murray
Pamela Trucano
Alex Wengart

Banana Boat Productions
City Of Pasadena
City Of San Dimas
City Of La Verne
CSUN Music Department
Entertainment Industry Development Corporation (EIDC)
Foundation For Early Childhood Development
National Center On Deafness
Necessary Evil
Pasadena Water & Power Department
St. Paul Lutheran Pre-School, Los Angeles
Charles Thomas - Environmental Consultant
Warrenwood Sound Studios

GOOD MACHINE

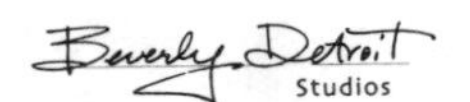

BUF

AMERICAN HUMANE ASSOCIATION MONITORED THE ANIMAL ACTION. NO ANIMAL WAS HARMED. SCENES APPEARING TO PLACE ANIMALS IN A JEOPARDY WERE SIMULATED.AHA 00085